# PURE
# SIN

# PURE
# SIN
## A PRIVILEGE NOVEL

BY

# KATE BRIAN

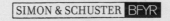
SIMON & SCHUSTER BFYR

New York   London   Toronto   Sydney

An imprint of Simon & Schuster Children's Publishing Division
1230 Avenue of the Americas, New York, NY 10020

 is a trademark of
Simon & Schuster, Inc.
For information about special discounts for bulk purchases,
please contact Simon & Schuster Special Sales at 1-866-506-1949 or
business@simonandschuster.com.
The Simon & Schuster Speakers Bureau can bring authors to your live
event. For more information or to book an event, contact the
Simon & Schuster Speakers Bureau at 1-866-248-3049 or visit our
website at www.simonspeakers.com.

Produced by Alloy Entertainment
151 West 26th Street, New York, NY 10001

Book design by Andrea C. Uva
The text of this book was set in Adobe Garamond.
Manufactured in the United States of America
2 4 6 8 10 9 7 5 3 1

Library of Congress Control Number: 2010932448
ISBN 978-1-4424-0786-2
ISBN 978-1-4424-0787-9 (eBook)

FIRST
EDITION

*For Matt and Brady*

# THE LIFE

*This is the life.*

Ariana Osgood sighed contentedly as she settled back into the strong arms of her boyfriend, Palmer Liriano, on a beautiful November morning. Outside the floor-to-ceiling windows at the Hill, the sky was a solid, bright blue, the trees along the banks of the Potomac a cheerful autumn mélange of oranges, reds, and golds. It was Friday, and after a long week of midterms and constant study groups, Palmer and Ariana had decided to spend their breakfast period in the junior and senior lounge, rather than the dining hall, so that they could snag some precious alone time. Ariana took a breath and relished the moment. This was what she had worked so hard for all these months—all these *years*. She was finally where she wanted to be. She had the prestigious school, the gorgeous boyfriend, the popular friends she was meant to have. But above all, she was free.

*Free.*

Ariana's skin tingled as the word passed through her mind, and she shivered slightly against Palmer's chest.

"You cold?" he asked, nuzzling her ear from behind. His early-morning voice was a pleasant, comforting rumble. "You can wear my jacket if you want."

Ariana nodded, then looked over her shoulder at him and touched her nose to his. Up close his green eyes were even more stunning, flecked with gold and blue. But even better was the way they shone when he looked at her. As if he couldn't believe how lucky he was to be with her. The most sought-after guy in school wanted *her*.

Palmer shrugged out of his navy blue Atherton-Pryce Hall blazer and held it open. Ariana slipped her arms into the sleeves. She wasn't cold, but she knew that walking around campus in his jacket would make her feel even more perfect, more secure. All the girls at APH would eye her with envy. It would solidify her as Palmer's girl. Everyone would know they were together. The thought made Ariana giggle with pleasure.

"What's so funny?" Palmer asked, placing his hands on her shoulders.

"Nothing. Just happy," Ariana said.

"Me too," Palmer replied matter-of-factly.

"Nice, isn't it?" Ariana asked, tucking her short, auburn hair behind her ear.

He grinned. "Very."

He touched his lips to hers, and they were still locked in a deep kiss when several of their friends dropped into the chairs around them.

"Break it up, dudes. There are virgins present," Landon Jacobs said, jerking his head toward Adam Lazzerri as he sat on the couch across from Ariana and Palmer.

Adam placed both hands over his heart, pretending to be wounded. "Maybe I haven't hooked up on every continent like *some* people, but I do okay."

Maria Stanzini groaned as she perched on the edge of the couch next to Landon. "Must our conversations always come back to Landon's many conquests?" she asked, taking a sip of her double espresso. Her light blue APH-issue button-down was slightly rumpled, her gold-and-gray-striped tie loose around her neck, but she still managed to look beautiful. Her light brown hair was back in a ponytail, with a few loose locks grazing her sharp cheekbones.

"What're you guys doing here?" Palmer asked in an annoyed tone. Ariana smiled, loving that he valued his time with her so much that it made him forget his manners.

"Soomie ordered those awful runny eggs again," Maria said, disgusted, sticking the tip of her tongue between her teeth. "I could *not* sit there a moment longer and watch her eat them."

"So gross." Adam shuddered.

"But if you guys are gonna nauseate me with talk of skeevy international hook-ups, I might as well just go back to my room," Maria added, turning her knees away from Landon.

Ariana shot Maria a sympathetic glance. As the only person on campus who knew about Maria and Landon's secret relationship— and as a person who'd just come out of the relationship closet with her own secret boyfriend—Ariana felt Maria's pain. It couldn't be easy being the clandestine girlfriend of a worldwide popstar-playboy. Of course, the playboy thing was a fabrication for the benefit of the fans and the press. At least, Ariana hoped it was, for Maria's sake.

The guys began to question Landon about the girl he'd supposedly hooked up with in Australia over the summer, prompting Maria to break out her iPod. Ariana eyed Lexa and her boyfriend, Conrad Royce, as they joined the group. They had their arms wrapped around each other, and each toted a coffee in their free hand. Conrad whispered something in Lexa's ear. She tipped her face up to look at him and smiled, her long dark hair tumbling down her back.

*Perfection,* Ariana thought. Lexa seemed happy and completely normal, which was a huge relief. Not many girls would have been able to hold it together after witnessing a friend kill another so-called friend in self-defense—and then help bury the body in her very own backyard. Luckily, Lexa was proving to be more resilient than most. In the past week she hadn't mentioned that fateful night to Ariana once.

Which made it a lot easier for Ariana to focus on other things. Like scouring the papers for any mention of Kiran Hayes's disappearance, or of a body washing up on the shore of the Potomac. As of that morning's *Washington Post,* there was still no such news. Which was another reason Ariana felt so very relaxed.

"What's up, gents?" Jasper Montgomery asked, walking over and dropping onto the couch next to Ariana. A leg of Jasper's dark gray wool pants scratched up against the bare stretch of thigh beneath her plaid skirt. Instantly her skin began to itch, and she moved her leg away.

"Ugh, Another text," Jasper muttered, looking at his cell. "I rue the day my mother figured out how to use modern technology."

"What's she bugging you about?" Adam asked Jasper.

"Travel plans for parents' weekend," Jasper replied, his thumbs moving rapidly over his keyboard. "She wants me to try out various hotel rooms this week and let them know which one they should stay in. She has a checklist for me. Quality of concierge service, promptness of room service, size of whirlpool bath . . ."

"Staying in hotels all week sounds like a good deal to me," Landon said. He tossed a bit of croissant in the air, leaned back, and caught it in his mouth. When he sat up again, his long brown bangs fell perfectly over his right eye. "I'll do it if you won't."

He ever so slightly nudged Maria's foot with his own, clearly thinking of some alone time for the two of them. Maria pushed her light brown ponytail over her shoulder and edged farther away from him.

"I don't know, Landon," Ariana said. "We might be otherwise occupied this week."

Adam, Landon, Jasper, and Ariana exchanged glances. They were four of the five candidates who were up for initiation in Stone and Grave, an exclusive secret society on campus. They had just gotten through hell week, so initiation had to be right around the corner. The question was when, exactly, would it take place? Lexa was the president of their chapter, so she clearly knew the answer to that question, as did Palmer, who was her number two, and Conrad, who was the guys' pledge educator. Even Maria was probably aware. Only the newbies had no clue what to expect.

"So, Adam, are your parents coming to parents' weekend?" Palmer asked, deftly changing the subject. "It'd be great to see them."

"Yup. They're making it their one vacation this year." As one of the few scholarship students at Atherton-Pryce, Adam was the only person in their group whose family didn't own villas and condos and pieds-à-terre around the globe. "They're gonna do the whole monument and museum thing while they're out here. What about you?"

"Of course," Palmer said. "My dad loves being here, and it's a great photo op for a congressperson," he joked. "Right, Lex?"

Lexa blinked. "Oh yeah. My mom and Senator Greene will be here, smiling for the cameras. I can't remember the last time they were at the Foxhall Road house."

"Are we still having brunch at your place that Sunday, Lex?" Maria asked.

Lexa glanced briefly at Ariana. Ariana knew what she was thinking: It would be the first time she and Ariana had been back to the house since Kaitlynn's death. Of course, as far as their friends were concerned, Lillian Oswald, née Kaitlynn Nottingham, had simply left school, unable to handle the workload.

Ariana waited for Lexa to flinch, but she just smiled. "Of course!" Lexa said brightly. "You all received your invites, right? My mother has a new chef, and she's just dying to trot him out."

As everyone discussed the menu, Ariana let herself relax. She was looking for problems where there were none. After all she'd been through in the past few years, no one could blame her for that.

"I just asked my mom, and she says they'd be delighted," Jasper said, tilting his phone. "Of course, she'll probably text back again to make sure you have enough guest towels to accommodate her. You guys are really going to *love* her," he added facetiously.

Ariana and the others laughed.

"I was kind of looking forward to meeting Lillian's family," Palmer said. "After how cagey she was about who they are. Kind of sucks that she bailed."

Ariana glanced at Lexa, who looked back at her furtively.

"Yes, well, if you can't handle the pressure of APH, I guess you shouldn't be at APH," Ariana said blithely. "*I* can't wait to meet Maria's parents. They look so glam in all your pictures."

"You won't be disappointed," Lexa put in, shooting Ariana a grateful look. "They *define* glam."

"They do have their moments," Maria said with a modest smile. "Personally, I'd like to meet Ana's infamous grandmother. I've never known anyone who had to check in with home as often as you do, A."

Ariana lifted one shoulder, pretending the every-other-day phone calls to Briana Leigh Covington's grandmother were just a matter of course, rather than sheer torture.

"She's just trying to honor my dad by looking out for me," she said. "But unfortunately, you won't get to meet her. She's too frail to travel."

*Thank goodness,* Ariana added silently. *Because if she ever did show up on this campus, she'd notice that I am not, in fact, her granddaughter.*

The real Briana Leigh Covington had been cremated in Ariana's name several months back, after Ariana had drowned her in order to steal her identity. Ariana swallowed hard, resolving not to think about it. That part of her life was behind her. All the unpleasantness. All the death. All of it. From now on, there was no need for any of it. She was really, truly Briana Leigh Covington. And no one would ever know otherwise.

"That sucks," Palmer said, giving her a squeeze. "I was looking forward to grilling her about your toddler years."

"Now *that* would have been interesting," Jasper added with a smirk.

"Yeah, so not going to happen," Ariana deadpanned.

The others laughed as the bell rang, signaling the end of the breakfast period.

"Do you want your jacket back?" Ariana asked Palmer.

"Keep it," he said. "It's kinda sexy, you wearing my clothes."

Then he pulled Ariana to him and kissed her. Ariana's eyes fluttered closed as she sunk into him, the rest of the world completely fading away. Palmer slipped his hand up her arm and over her shoulder until he was cupping her cheek. Ariana heard everyone else file out of the room, but still she couldn't pull herself away. Then an empty paper cup suddenly hit her in the head.

"Hey!" Palmer protested with a laugh.

"I told you! Virgins are present!" Landon protested, throwing his hands out.

"Yeah, come on, sluts. We're going to be late for class," Conrad put in with a laugh.

Palmer shrugged and reached for both of Ariana's hands, hoisting her off the couch. She had to step over Jasper's feet to get around the table. He was the only one of their group who hadn't moved. Ariana glanced back at him as they headed for the door, expecting to find him still furiously texting, but he wasn't.

Instead he was looking directly at her. And he had a smirk on his handsome face that was completely unreadable.

# INITIATION

"Oh, crap," Tahira Al-Mahmood said, pausing outside as the dining hall door slammed shut behind her and Ariana. "I was going to grab a couple of those éclairs to take back to my room. I can't study without sugar."

She started to turn around, but Ariana stopped her, placing her hand on Tahira's arm. Quinn, Ariana's favorite sophomore lackey, was walking toward them, her red ponytail swinging jauntily.

"Hey, Quinn," Ariana said.

"What's up," Quinn said with a bright smile. She clutched her books to her chest.

"Tahira would like an éclair. Would you mind running in and getting one for her?" Ariana asked.

Quinn blinked, clearly confused. Ariana knew why. Quinn normally acted as coffee gopher for Lexa, Ariana, Maria, and Soomie, but had never been sent on an errand for Tahira before. Even Tahira looked stunned.

"Is there a problem?" Ariana asked.

"No. Of course not," Quinn answered quickly. She knew that questioning orders would not be good for her position at APH, nor for her chances of making Stone and Grave the following year. "I'll be right back."

"Okay, what was that?" Tahira said as Quinn disappeared through the door. She shoved her hands into the pockets of her white coat, her diamond nose ring twinkling under the doorway light. "Lexa's gonna freak."

"No, she won't," Ariana said, holding herself against a cold breeze. "Things are different now."

It was a simple statement for a simple truth. Tahira and Ariana were the only two girls being initiated into Stone and Grave. During their pledge period, Ariana had grown close to Tahira. That made her part of the group, without question.

"If you say so," Tahira said, looking less than confident for the first time since Ariana had met her.

"Here you go!" Quinn opened the door and handed Tahira a wax-paper bag full of pastry. "Anything else?" she asked, looking only at Tahira.

"No. That'll be all," Tahira said, amused.

Quinn smiled and went back inside, leaving Ariana and Tahira alone to stroll across campus.

"So, have I mentioned I'm totally jealous of you?" Tahira asked, shaking her wavy dark hair back as she peeked inside her pastry bag. "I would pretty much kill to have a single right now."

Ariana bit down on her tongue to keep from laughing at the irony of that statement. "It *is* the greatest thing ever."

"I'll bet," Tahira said, her dark eyes wide. "I love Allison, but if I could get her to disappear, I would. I need some more space. Back home I have an entire wing *and* my own pool. Here I don't even have my own bathroom. Plus she's been kind of pissy ever since she got thrown out of S and G. I mean, I was pissed too, you know, but at some point it's just like . . . get over it already."

"Totally," Ariana replied. "Do you think she's jealous of you?"

"She's jealous of all of us," Tahira confirmed. "Sometimes I think that if you don't get in to S and G, you shouldn't be allowed to live in Privilege House. I mean, it's just so annoying. For both of us. There's all this stuff I can't talk about, and she's irritated because she thinks I'm being a bad friend. It's unnecessarily hard."

Ariana smiled to herself, thinking how odd it was to be having a heart-to-heart with a girl who, just a couple of months ago, was her sworn enemy. "Maybe you two should just—"

Ariana's advice died on her lips when she heard footsteps rushing up behind them. She glanced at Tahira, and they both froze.

Suddenly a thin black sack came down over Ariana's head. Her heart fluttered with excitement as two firm hands gripped her arms and yanked her off the pathway into the evergreen bushes alongside.

This was it. Initiation.

"Let's go, plebe," a gruff voice growled in her ear.

# INTERESTING DEVELOPMENT

Ariana's shoes crunched over dried, dead grass, and the group stopped while someone opened a heavy, creaking door. As Ariana was manhandled down a set of shallow concrete steps, she was careful to maintain her balance to keep from tripping. Now that she and the other pledges knew that the Tombs were located in the basement of the APH library, being taken there under black hoods seemed pointless, but she understood that it was all part of the tradition. At the bottom of the steps she started to turn to the left, as usual, but this time, she was yanked to the right.

Okay. This was new. Ariana's heart pounded in earnest as they shuffled along the concrete floor. The two Stone and Grave brothers who led her kept bumping into her hips as if they were hemmed in on both sides by a narrow hallway. They paused again, and frigid air rushed in all around her. There was a lot of whispering and shuffling, followed by a series of odd squeals and wails, like several rusty latches opening. Ariana's throat was dry.

Finally, Ariana was shoved forward, and the brothers let go. Wherever they had left her, it was freezing. Her wool coat did nothing to ward off the chill. Then someone came forward and ripped that coat off her shoulders.

"Strip!" dozens of voices shouted.

"Here we go."

Ariana recognized Jasper's voice. He must have been mere inches from her in the darkness.

"Strip!" the brothers shouted again.

Shaking, Ariana removed her heeled boots and unbuttoned her jeans. As she bent to tug them off her heels, she bumped into Jasper and staggered forward. Goosebumps popped up all over her legs as she fought for her footing. She took a breath. So what if dozens of her friends were watching this ridiculous, humiliating display? So what if they were laughing at her in the dark? It was all for a good cause. Removing her V-neck cashmere sweater without taking her black hood with it proved to be a bit more difficult, but she managed, dropping the sweater on the ground at her feet. As soon as she was down to her bra and underwear, someone stepped forward and brought a familiarly itchy burlap sack down over her head, cinching it around her waist with a rope.

She was dying to scratch the openings around her neck and elbows. But she knew better than to move.

*Just breathe,* she told herself. *This will be the last time you have to wear this thing.*

A pair of strong hands came down on her shoulders suddenly and turned her around. She could feel someone moving next to her and assumed Jasper was being directed in the same way. When the bags were removed from their heads, would they be facing the brethren? Would this all be over soon? Ariana hoped that Palmer would be right in front of her so she could see him. So she could be looking at him when they performed the rite that would make them members.

Then, out of nowhere, someone grabbed Ariana's hands and wrenched them behind her back. This, too, was new. Her wrists were tied together with some kind of thick cord that, when pulled tight, sent a stabbing pain into her upper arms. The black sacks were ripped off, and Ariana's heart hit her throat. She wasn't looking into the warm, loving eyes of her boyfriend. Instead, she was looking down at a plain wooden coffin. Actually there were three coffins, set down in deep ditches in the dirt, which had been exposed thanks to a huge hole in the cement floor. She was in a room she had never seen before. More like a cavern, really. The walls were curved like a dome and made of jagged black rock. The room was circular, but the hole in the floor was a perfect rectangle. Low candles flickered all around the hole, but otherwise there was no light in the cavern, and no sign of life.

Where was Palmer? Where were the rest of the Stone and Grave members? The brothers that had brought them here? Ariana looked at Jasper, alarmed.

"What the—" He was cut off when someone shoved him from behind. He fell into the coffin in front of them with a thud. Terror seized Ariana, but she didn't have time to react. A foot hit her in the small of the back, and suddenly she was free-falling, face-first, with no way to stop herself. She landed right on top of Jasper, clunking heads with him. Stars burst in front of her eyes, almost blacking out her vision.

"That's gonna leave a mark," Jasper said, wincing.

"How can you joke at a time like this?" Ariana hissed. She flipped over onto her back as best she could in the small space, stabbing Jasper's ribs with her elbow before crushing both arms beneath her. She looked up to see the coffin lid being lowered over them.

"No!" she screamed, and heard Tahira shout out as well, her voice muffled. "Stop!"

"Silence!" someone growled.

And then, all was dark.

"Well," Jasper whispered, his lips grazing her earlobe. "This just got interesting."

# NAUGHTINESS

*Trapped. I'm trapped. I'm trapped inside a coffin in the ground in a cellar, and no one knows I'm here.*

The bottom of the coffin was hard and cold against her shoulder, and pain radiated up her spine, into the base of her skull. All she could hear was her pulse rushing in her ears, and the steady sound of Jasper's breathing.

*Don't be stupid, Ariana. Tons of people know you're here. Palmer, Lexa, Maria, Soomie, Conrad, April, Rob, Hunter . . . and certainly Jasper, every inch of whose body is touching yours. He couldn't exactly miss you, could he?*

Ariana tried to take a deep breath, but the air in the coffin was thick with humidity and the choking scents of mold and dirt. She turned her head toward the ceiling and coughed, struggling for air.

*But no one knows I'm* here. *Me. Ariana Osgood. No one knows where*

*I am. I could die here and no one would know. Not my mother or my father or—*

*They already think you're dead, you idiot! Shut up and stop heaving! You're going to use up all the oxygen!*

"Ana?"

Ariana flinched at the sound of Jasper's voice. She slammed her head into the lid of the coffin, reinjuring the exact spot where she'd hit Jasper. The pain exploded all over again.

"What?" she said through her teeth.

"Are you okay?" Jasper asked. "You do know there are air holes in this thing, right? We have enough oxygen."

"Are you sure?" Ariana asked, sounding irritatingly pathetic.

"I promise," Jasper assured her calmly.

Ariana's right arm was screaming from bearing all her weight. She tried to squirm into a new position and rest more squarely on her back, but she succeeded only in pressing her shoulder blades together so tightly that she pulled a muscle—and flattened Jasper against the wall.

"Ow. Okay, there is someone else in here with you, you know," Jasper said.

"Sorry," Ariana went back to her former position. "And speaking of which, weren't there three coffins in the ground?"

"So?" Jasper said.

"So? Do the math. There are five of us. Which one of us got a coffin all to themselves?" Ariana whispered. "My best friend is the president, and my boyfriend is second in line. Where the hell are my perks?"

Jasper laughed. "Perhaps you're not as significant as you think you are."

Ariana's face burned at the insult, and for the first time she was grateful for the pitch darkness.

"Besides," he added, his tone more placating. "Think about it. Would you really want to be in here alone?"

Ariana considered this. The boy had a point. If he weren't there to distract her, she'd probably be having an acute panic attack.

"How long have we been in here, anyway?" she asked. "An hour? Three hours? When are they going to let us out already?"

"Ana, we've only been in here about fifteen minutes," Jasper said, sounding amused.

"What? That's not possible," Ariana whispered.

"I've been counting the seconds since they closed the coffin," Jasper replied matter-of-factly. "We're at exactly nine hundred and four."

Ariana scoffed. "You have not."

"Yes. I have."

"That is so not possible," Ariana replied. Jasper said nothing. His breath was minty fresh on her face. "You can do that?" she asked finally.

"I can do lots of things."

She felt him shift, his cheek pressing against hers as he leaned forward. For a brief moment she was sure he was trying to kiss her. Unbidden, her skin sizzled and her face burned. But then she felt his fingers on her hip.

"Wait," she said slowly, realizing what this meant. "You got your hands free."

"Ta-da," Jasper said, tapping her hip with his fingers.

"How did you do that?" she asked.

"Not important." Jasper shook his head slightly and his nose brushed hers. Ariana's heart seized, and she suddenly felt light-headed.

*I am not attracted to Jasper,* she told herself. *It's just all this . . . touching. And lack of air.*

"Here. Let me get yours," Jasper said, making a move.

"Wait," Ariana said. "Won't they be mad if we're untied when they let us out of here?"

"I think they'll be impressed with our ingenuity," Jasper replied. "Here."

He bent his right elbow, then straightened his arm out so that it rested in the open space between her neck and the bottom of the coffin. Then he slid it down under her shoulder, so that it was pinned beneath her. His arm continued to travel down, while Ariana twisted and adjusted, doing her best to lift her weight off of it and help him along, until his hand found hers behind her back. At that moment, her weight tipped her forward over his forearm, and suddenly her whole body was pressed against his. Her face buried itself in the spot between his shoulder and his neck. If she pursed her lips, she could have kissed his skin.

"Almost there," Jasper whispered, his voice husky.

His left arm was around her now, pulling her, impossibly, even closer to him. His body was wiry and strong. Stronger than she would have thought just by looking at him. As he struggled to blindly untie the cord that bound her hands, his breath was hot and labored on the back of her neck.

"How's it going?" she said, because she felt she had to say something.

"I think I've . . . yes. I've got it," Jasper whispered.

She felt a jerk and the cord slipped free.

"Thanks," she breathed.

"Any time."

Jasper leaned backward, and the space between them suddenly felt like a chasm. With some effort, Ariana brought her hands in front of her. She folded them at chest level and Jasper did the same. Now the two pledges were curled, knees touching, hands touching, foreheads touching, perfect mirror images.

"So," he said, his breath warm and comforting against her face, "what do we do now?"

"I don't know," she said quietly. "What do you want to do?"

"I think you already know the answer to that question."

Ariana's heart skipped a startled beat. "Jasper, I—"

"Kidding!" he said with a laugh. "For someone so smart, you sure are gullible."

Ariana's face burned anew. She was just about to tell him off when there was a sudden, deafening crack, and the coffin was wrenched open.

Ariana blinked, her eyes throbbing with pain at the sudden tidal wave of light. She looked up, right into the ashen face of Palmer Liriano.

"Sonofa—"

Suddenly Ariana saw herself and Jasper in her mind's eye and realized what they must look like to Palmer, half-naked and curled into each other.

"Palmer, I—" Ariana sat up, kneeing Jasper right in the groin. He curled into a ball, muttering curses.

"How the hell did you two get your hands free?" he blurted.

Ariana let out a sigh, relieved that Palmer was only upset that she and Jasper had untied themselves.

"No talking!" Conrad hissed, coming over to stand next to Palmer.

Gritting his teeth, Palmer reached down for Ariana with both hands. She grasped his forearms as he hauled her up, and tripped into him once her feet hit the cold floor.

Conrad helped Jasper out of the coffin. He doubled over, still catching his breath. Ariana glanced to the right and saw that Tahira and Adam had emerged from the second coffin. It was Landon who had been all alone in his. Probably, Ariana realized, because he was supposed to be locked in with Kaitlynn.

"Stand up, brother," Conrad whispered to Jasper, finally slapping him on the back.

Jasper took a deep breath, blew it out, and managed to stand up semistraight. As soon as he did, dozens of new candles lit up the room as the rest of the Stone and Grave brotherhood emerged from the shadows. Ariana's heart lifted.

"Welcome, brothers and sisters, to the Stone and Grave!"

# DESTROYED

The cool, satiny insides of her black Stone and Grave robe were even more heavenly than Ariana had imagined, especially after the torture of the burlap sack. As she knelt in front of a wide, stone altar, with Lexa standing before her, she could hardly contain her giddiness. This was it. She was finally going to be an official member of Stone and Grave.

Tahira knelt down beside her, giving her a secret smile. Ariana grinned back as Jasper knelt at her other side. It was all happening.

Standing behind their personal gravestones were the rest of the members of Stone and Grave. Ariana could see Palmer, stationed behind his gray stone that read "Starbuck," his hands folded reverently in front of him. His face was expressionless at first, but when she met his gaze he smiled, ever so briefly. It was a private, proud smile, and it warmed Ariana from the inside out.

"Brothers and sisters, tonight we welcome five worthy members into our family," Lexa began, her voice ringing out loud and clear in the silent room. Her dark hair gleamed in the candlelight. "Each person gathered here has proven him or herself to be a valuable member of Stone and Grave, but let us not forget the potential we have lost. A moment of silence for Brigit Rhygstead."

Ariana bowed her head, surprised by the sudden mention of her friend, who had died at the hands of Kaitlynn Nottingham. Lexa did not mention Lillian Oswald.

"Thank you," Lexa said, lifting her face. "And now, we will begin our ritual."

She turned and lifted a gray stone bowl from atop the altar. Soomie walked over and stood next to her, holding something small and glittery in her palm. April Coorigan and Conrad, the pledge group's educators, joined them, their robes billowing as they moved. Conrad lifted three headstones from behind the altar, while April lifted two. Palmer stepped forward and slid a long silver needle off the surface as well. Its sharp point glinted in the candlelight. Ariana's heart caught. What, exactly, did they plan to do with that?

Together, Lexa, Palmer, and Soomie approached Jasper.

"Brother, your name, from this moment on, is Amory Blaine," Lexa said. Amory Blaine. The preppy, lazy, yet charming hero of *This Side of Paradise*. What a perfect name for Jasper. Still, Ariana felt a slight twinge of disappointment. She had thought they would have the chance to choose their own names. Hopefully she wouldn't be saddled with something lame and predictable out of some Brontë novel.

From her palm, Soomie plucked a graphite-encrusted pin and held it up in the candlelight. The gray stones formed a small skull. She leaned down and fastened the pin to Jasper's robe, then stepped back again.

"Hold out your hand," Lexa instructed.

Jasper did as he was told without hesitation. Lexa held the bowl beneath his hand as Palmer took the silver needle and pricked Jasper's pointer finger with it. A bead of dark red blood emerged. Palmer tilted Jasper's hand and squeezed his finger, so that a few drops of blood hit the bowl.

"Ugh. Sick," Tahira whispered. Ariana barely blinked. Blood had no effect on her.

Palmer, Conrad, April, and Soomie all looked at Lexa expectantly. Ariana's eyes darted to her friend's face. Lexa was staring down at the bowl, her skin unnaturally waxy and practically translucent. Her eyes were as wide as moons.

Suddenly Ariana's heart started to race. What was wrong with Lexa?

"Sister Becky Sharp?" Palmer prompted her.

Lexa looked up at him, startled, as if she'd forgotten he was there—forgotten that any of them were there. Ariana wished she could pull her friend aside and talk to her. Was it the blood? Was she thinking about Kaitlynn's death?

Then Lexa cleared her throat. She swung her hair back over her shoulders and smiled, taking a deep breath as if she was just gathering herself together.

Ariana let out a sigh of relied. *That's my girl,* she thought.

"By adding your blood to our sacred vessel, you swear an oath to us," Lexa said to Jasper. "Repeat after me. I, Jasper Montgomery, do hereby accept the name of Amory Blaine and forevermore pledge my life and soul to the brotherhood of Stone and Grave."

After Jasper repeated the oath, Lexa, Palmer, and April moved to stand in front of Ariana. Conrad placed Jasper's headstone in front of him for the first time.

"Sister," Lexa said, shaking her hair back and looking Ariana in the eye. "Your name, from this moment on, will be Portia."

A thrill of satisfaction went through Ariana, and she grinned up at Lexa. She adored Portia, the strong, beautiful heroine of *The Merchant of Venice*. If she'd been allowed to choose for herself, she couldn't have picked better. Willingly, Ariana held out her hand above Lexa's stone vessel. She could see the tiny pool of blood Jasper had left at the bottom of the bowl. Palmer reached out and pricked her finger. He squeezed out a few drops of her blood, adding it to Jasper's in the bowl.

"By adding your blood to our sacred vessel, you swear an oath to us," Lexa said. "Repeat after me. I, Briana Leigh Covington, do hereby accept the name of Portia and forevermore pledge my life and soul to the brotherhood of Stone and Grave."

"I, Briana Leigh Covington, do hereby accept the name of Portia and forevermore pledge my life and soul to the brotherhood of Stone and Grave."

Palmer smiled over Lexa's shoulder, and Ariana felt a burst of pure joy. Soomie stepped forward and affixed her Stone and Grave pin to her robe, and then April placed her headstone in front of her. As the group moved on to Tahira, Ariana tilted the pin toward her.

She had done it. Finally, *finally*, she was an official member of one of the most influential secret societies in the country, which meant that the whole world was at her fingertips.

# A VERY WEALTHY YOUNG LADY

"I'm so glad you like your name," Lexa said as she and Ariana walked toward the dining hall late on Sunday morning. They had been up most of the night, partying with the rest of the Stone and Grave members, and were barely going to make it to breakfast before the dining hall closed. "I struggled hardest with yours because I wanted to get it just right."

"Really?" Ariana said, blushing. "Thanks for working so hard on it."

Lexa grinned and took her arm. "What are best friends for?"

They had just reached the door of the dining hall when Maria and Landon came striding around the corner, their heads so close together they were practically kissing.

"Dude," Landon said, shoving Maria away from him.

Ariana glanced at Lexa to see if she noticed anything odd, but Lexa merely smiled.

"Good morning. Are you two coming or going?" she asked them.

"Coming. I mean, uh, going," Landon said, scratching the back of his neck. "We just, uh, ate."

Maria rolled her eyes. "Excuse him. Someone's still a little hungover from last night."

"Rock star can't party like a rock star, huh?" Ariana joked.

Landon blushed, hanging his head as he glanced at Maria guiltily from under his bangs.

"I'm glad I bumped into you guys," Maria said, without a trace of Landon's awkwardness. She had her hand inside her bag and was rooting around for something. "Now I can give you these."

She extracted three dark gray, oblong envelopes from her bag and handed one to each of them.

"What are they?" Ariana asked.

"Invitations," Maria replied, glancing around. The campus was quiet, as it usually was on Sundays, with people either sleeping in or heading out for shopping sprees or to visit family. Except for a couple of joggers at the far end of the sunlit quad, there was no one in sight. "To the Stone and Grave Ball at the end of next week. My parents offered to host."

"Cool," Landon said.

"Not to look a gift invitation in the mouth, but didn't we celebrate last night?" Ariana asked, tucking hers into her bag.

"Yes, but this is much bigger," Maria told them. "All the local Stone and Grave chapters attend. Everyone from all the private schools in Virginia and Maryland will be there, as well of some of the most influential alumni. We're talking serious networking possibilities."

"How do you think she got to tour with the Boston Ballet last summer?" Lexa put in.

Ariana frowned, impressed. "All right. I'm in."

"Of course you're in," Maria said, reaching back to tug the band from her ponytail. Her hair tumbled over her shoulders. "It's an *intense* party."

Ariana saw Landon reach up automatically to touch her hair. Maria froze and Landon flinched, pulling his hand back. It was all Ariana could do to keep from groaning in frustration. Why didn't they just let the proverbial cat out of its stifling bag already? Who cared if the kids at school knew? They could still keep the secret from Maria's dad, who'd forbidden her to date.

"Oh, and there's a dress code," Lexa said, slipping her invite into her handbag and reaching for the door. "Everyone has to wear gray or black."

"That's not very festive," Ariana said. She'd always hated the tendency of the girls at Easton to wear black to parties. New York and Connecticut bashes always ended up looking like upscale funerals. And despite recent events, Ariana was in no mood for a funeral. "I don't even own a black dress."

"Shopping spree!" Lexa squealed as Maria strode off, Landon loping a few paces behind. "Come on. Let's get inside before all the pancakes are gone."

Ariana's cell phone rang. Lexa paused in front of the door, waiting for Ariana to extract the phone from her bag. The number had a Texas area code, but it wasn't one of the Covingtons' numbers. She took a few steps away from the door to let April and Hunter—another couple of Stone and Grave stragglers—inside.

"Hello?" she said, as Lexa followed her, keeping a polite distance.

"Miss Covington? This is Leon Jessup, attorney at law," a gruff voice greeted her.

"Uh . . . hello," Ariana replied, confused.

"I'm very sorry to be the one to tell you, but your grandmother has passed away."

Ariana simply stared at her phone, dumbfounded. Briana Leigh's grandmother had died? Lexa eyed her with curiosity, and suddenly Ariana remembered the role she had to play here—that of a girl who had just found out that the only family member she had left in the world had just died.

"Miss Covington?" Jessup said.

"Yes," Ariana said. She turned her profile to Lexa and gripped a low-hanging branch on an elm tree for support. She knew she should be crying, but she couldn't seem to summon any tears for the old woman. "Yes, I'm here. I'm just . . . stunned. What happened?"

"It was peaceful," the man replied. "She passed away during the night. I'm very sorry for your loss."

"I can't believe this is happening." Ariana squeezed her eyes closed, forcing herself to think back to one of the worst days in her own life—the day of her own funeral. She'd watched her mother and father sob over the ashes they thought were hers. She felt a choking sob hit her throat, and tears stung her eyes. Lexa stepped closer and took her hand.

*What is it?* she mouthed.

"My grandmother," Ariana whispered.

Lexa covered her mouth with her free hand.

"I know this is short notice, but I'm flying to DC tomorrow so that you can sign the paperwork," Jessup said, all business.

"The paperwork?" Ariana repeated. A tear spilled over onto her cheek, and she would have wiped it away if Lexa weren't crushing her fingers in her grip.

"Yes. So that you can receive your inheritance," Jessup said impatiently.

"What?" Ariana blurted. Lexa was now alarmed. She searched Ariana's face, as if looking for some kind of answer as to what, exactly, was going on. Ariana's pulse raced like mad. "But I thought that was supposed to be held in trust until I was twenty-five."

"I don't know anything about that," Jessup said. Ariana could hear papers rustling in the background. "As far as your grandmother's estate is concerned, it all goes to you upon her death, and your parents' estate is to be released to you as well. As of three o'clock this morning, Miss Covington, you are a very wealthy young lady."

Ariana looked at Lexa, who was clearly desperate for the exact details. It took every single ounce of control and strength and sheer will inside of Ariana to appear as devastated as a truly dedicated grand-daughter would have felt at that moment—to keep from twirling in a circle on the grass, throwing her head back, and singing at the top of her lungs.

Because she wasn't Briana Leigh Covington. Not in her heart of hearts. Down deep, she would always be Ariana Osgood. And thanks to good old Grandma Covington's timely kicking of the bucket, all of Ariana Osgood's fondest dreams were about to come true.

# FINE

"Are you going to go home for the funeral?" Lexa asked as the elevator rose to the top floor of Privilege House that evening. They'd spent the past few hours in the library with their American history study group, but Ariana had zoned out, daydreaming about what she was going to do with all her newfound money. But hearing Lexa's words, Ariana's heart dropped, as if the lift had suddenly taken a dive for the ground. She hadn't even considered the funeral—which she absolutely could not attend, because someone would undoubtedly notice she was not the real Briana Leigh.

"I don't know. The lawyer didn't mention any plans," Ariana replied, trying to keep voice steady.

"Do you want me to call him back for you?" Lexa said. "I understand if it's all too much."

"That's sweet, but don't worry about it," Ariana said, trying to think five steps ahead, trying to come up with a plan to get out of going to Texas. "I'll figure it out."

They exited the elevator and turned the corner into the hallway leading to their rooms.

"It's freezing in here," Ariana said, pulling her wool coat tighter around her body.

Lexa touched Ariana's arm, her eyes wide. "Why's the door to my room open?"

The two of them walked cautiously down the hall together. They found Maria standing just inside her and Lexa's room, wearing flannel pajama bottoms and an Atherton-Pryce sweatshirt, her arms folded as she kept an eye on a janitor, who was crouched to the floor. Wind whipped through the window across from the open door, where jagged broken edges of glass stuck out in all directions.

"What happened?" Ariana asked, taking a step into the room. Lexa hovered in the doorway.

"I wouldn't come any closer, miss," the janitor said over his shoulder. "There're glass shards everywhere."

"Some freshmen decided to play baseball in the dark. Apparently they didn't know their own strength," Maria said wryly.

Suddenly one of the shards fell loose from the pane and crashed to the floor, shattering into a million tiny pieces.

"I think . . . I'm going to—" Lexa gasped.

Ariana turned around. Lexa was as pale as milk. A second later, she fainted dead away.

"Lexa!" Maria cried, rushing over to her friend. Ariana ran to the bathroom and came back with a cool, wet towel. She placed it on Lexa's forehead. A moment later, her friend's green eyes fluttered open.

"Kaitlynn?" Lexa croaked, pointing limply to the window, where the janitor was sweeping up the last shards.

Ariana's heart crashed to her knees. The broken window. The shattered glass. This was how Kaitlynn died. Ariana fought the urge to curse aloud. This was not good. This was very, very not good.

"She must be disoriented," Ariana said to Maria, who had a panicked look on her face. "Lexa, are you okay?"

"Lex, what happened?" Maria asked, grabbing her friend's hand.

Ariana forced herself to breathe. Lexa could not lose it now. She simply couldn't. Not when everything was finally going Ariana's way.

"Do you have low blood sugar? You didn't eat very much at dinner," Ariana said before Lexa could answer. She stared at Lexa, silently begging her friend to keep her mouth shut.

"I think we should take you to the infirmary," Maria said worriedly. The janitor finished taping up the window and left the three girls alone in the room.

Slowly the room began to warm up, and color returned to Lexa's face. "No, I'm sure Ana's right." Lexa struggled to sit up. "Besides, I'm fine now. I swear," Lexa said, as Maria opened her mouth to protest.

Ariana forced a smile for Maria's benefit. The two girls helped Lexa into her bed and pulled the covers up tight around her chin.

"Are you sure you're okay? I can get you some food or call the nurse," Maria said, laying her hand across Lexa's forehead.

"Seriously, guys, I'm fine," Lexa said, waving Maria and Ariana away from her. "Thanks, but I just need some sleep."

"Do you want me to stay?" Ariana said uncertainly, her hand on the doorknob. "Or you could sleep in my room if you're worried about . . . the window."

Lexa shook her head. "I'm fine. Now shoo!" She closed her eyes and snuggled down on her pillow.

Ariana hesitated for a long moment and glanced at Maria. Maria shrugged, so Ariana exited, shutting the door quietly behind her. Once in the hallway, she sank to the floor and clutched her arms, drawing blood where her fingernails dug into her skin.

Sure, Lexa said she was fine. But people who were fine didn't faint at the sight of broken glass. And if Lexa wasn't fine, she could take everything Ariana had fought so hard for away with one ill-timed breakdown.

# CRISIS OF CONSCIENCE

The next morning, Ariana watched from her window as the weak November sun lit the facades of Atherton-Pryce Hall's redbrick buildings. Down below, Maria headed out in gray sweats and a pink fleece jacket, her toe shoes slung over her shoulder, walking briskly toward her early-morning workout in the dance studio. Once Maria turned the corner around the dining hall, Ariana went to the mirror on the back of her dorm room door. She mussed her hair a bit, trying to make it look as if she'd just woken up, then cinched her white silk robe and headed for the room Lexa and Maria shared at the end of the hall.

*Everything's going to be just fine,* she told herself as she padded silently along the thick carpeting. *She just needs a good talking-to.*

She paused in front of the closed dorm room door, took a deep breath, and knocked lightly.

"Come in!" Lexa said, her voice surprisingly bright.

Ariana opened the door and poked her head inside tentatively.

Lexa was already showered and dressed, her red sweater wrinkle free over boyfriend jeans and brown boots.

"You're up early," she said to Ariana with a smile.

"Not as early as you," Ariana replied.

"I have to do some last-minute cramming for my French test," Lexa said. "I'm gonna hit the library before breakfast. You wanna come?"

Ariana eyed her quizzically. Was this chipper thing for real? "Actually, I have to go into the city today. To meet with that lawyer," she said.

Lexa closed her eyes and brought her hand to her forehead. "That's right. I'm so sorry! Is there anything I can do?"

"No, thanks. I'll be fine," Ariana replied. "I just wanted to see how you were doing this morning. Are you feeling better?"

Lexa tilted her head as she fluffed her pillow two, five, then ten times. "Yeah. I am." She laughed in an embarrassed way, then lifted her folded blanket from her desk chair and spread it across her bed. "I was just overtired," she said, turning her back toward Ariana as she moved around the bottom of the bed, smoothing out the wrinkles. "You may not remember this about me, but when I get overtired, my whole system freaks out. And lately? I really haven't been sleeping a lot."

Ariana wondered if the real Briana Leigh would have remembered this tidbit about Lexa from their time together at equestrian camp as kids. Her guess was probably not. Briana Leigh was a tad too self-involved to recall details about other people.

"Oh," Ariana said, feeling slightly better as she click, click, clicked the stapler. "Well, how did you sleep last night?"

"Okay, I guess," Lexa said with a shrug. "At least, I definitely slept at some point, because I remember having a dream." She narrowed her eyes. "Something about my parents parachuting through the roof of my house. Isn't that weird?" Lexa laughed and then shook her head. "Anyway, any sleep at all is an improvement."

She stopped primping the bed, and turned to Ariana. "Honestly, don't worry about me. I'm totally fine. I just feel bad that I made you worry."

Ariana breathed a sigh of relief. Everything was okay. All Lexa had needed was a good night's sleep, and she was herself again.

"Oh, that's all right," she said.

Lexa unexpectedly wrapped Ariana in a hug. "Do you want me to come with you today? I'm sure I could make up the test."

"No, thanks. I'm sure it'll be fine. I just want to get it over with," Ariana replied, edging toward the door. "I'm going to go take a shower. I mean, as long as you're all right. . . ."

"Of course I'm all right," Lexa said, turning back toward her bed and smoothing out a wrinkle that wasn't there. "Why shouldn't I be all right? I mean, just because I aided and abetted a murder, and just because the dead body of my former friend who tried to kill me is buried in my backyard, and just because if anyone ever finds it we're both going to jail and my entire family will be ruined, I mean, why would any of that make me not all right?"

Ariana stopped with her hand on the doorknob. "Lexa?"

Suddenly Lexa sat down on her perfectly made bed, buried her face in her hands, and burst into tears.

*Oh, I am so very, very screwed,* Ariana thought.

Watching her friend blubber uncontrollably, Ariana's heart started to pound real terror through her veins. She breathed in and out, in and out, but it didn't help. The telltale gray dots started to prickle over her vision. She gripped her forearm in one hand and squeezed as hard as she could, trying to keep herself present. Trying to keep herself in the now.

Trying to keep herself from snapping.

*Breathe, Ariana. Just breathe.*

*In, one . . . two . . . three . . .*

*Out, one . . . two . . . three . . .*

*In, one . . . two . . . three . . .*

*Out, one . . . two . . . three . . .*

Her vision began to clear, and she took a step forward. "Lexa, listen, I know this is difficult, but it's all going to be okay."

"How?" Lexa blurted, lifting her face. "I can't stop thinking about it. I can't stop . . . seeing her face. You killed her, Ana. And I helped you hide it. That makes me an accessory."

Ariana gritted her teeth. It was never a good sign when people started talking in legal terms. It meant they were *thinking* in legal terms. Which meant they were considering bringing the law into it. Ariana could not have this.

"Lex, it was self-defense," Ariana said, sitting next to Lexa on the bed and taking her hand. "She was trying to kill you. Did you want me to let her do that?"

"No!" Lexa replied. "But if it *was* self-defense, then it should be fine. If we tell the police, they'll—"

"It's too late for that," Ariana said, squeezing her friend's hand. "We hid her body. We cleaned up your house. It's been two weeks. If we tell them now, it doesn't matter how we say it happened, we're going to look guilty."

"But—"

"There's no reason to cry over her, Lexa," Ariana said calmly. "The girl knew you were hiring a PI to look into her past. Clearly there was something she didn't want you to find. She came there to kill you. Do you understand that? The girl was psychotic."

Lexa's eyes were wide with terror, as if she expected Kaitlynn to burst through the door at any moment and try to take her life all over again.

"You and I are the only ones who know what happened that night," Ariana said, looking Lexa directly in the eye. "As long as we keep the secret between us, we'll be fine. You'll remain president of Stone and Grave, your dad will keep his job, and we'll both graduate and go on to wonderful things. But if we tell . . ."

She let the implication hang in the air. Lexa looked across the room at the photograph of her and her parents posing with the president, everyone wearing huge smiles. Ariana could practically see the gears working in her friend's mind as she realized anew what could happen. Her life, her father's political career, her future—all of it could be taken from her.

"You're right," Lexa said finally, sniffling as she looked down at her lap. "I don't know what I was thinking."

Ariana wrapped her arm around Lexa. "It's okay. So . . . no police?"

"No police," Lexa said.

"And no more freak-outs?" Ariana asked, holding her breath.

"No more freak-outs," Lexa promised. Then she turned and hugged Ariana with both arms. "Thank you so much, Ana. For saving my life."

"Of course," Ariana replied, closing her eyes as she hugged Lexa back. She had cleared this hurdle. Now all she could do was hope that Lexa kept her promises. "I would do it again in a heartbeat, Lexa," she added. "You're my best friend."

# A MOMENT OF HAPPINESS

When Ariana walked into the sunlit conference room at Jessup, Martin, and Falk, Leon Jessup was kicked back in one of the leather chairs around the glass-topped conference table, reading the local paper. He was a large man, broad and tall, his shoulders spilling over the sides of the wide chairback. In his mouth was a breath mint, which he rolled around on his tongue and occasionally bit down on. Behind him was a wall of rounded windows overlooking the Smithsonian Institution Building, where yellow school buses were lined up like limousines waiting outside the Academy Awards. The attorney didn't notice Ariana until she cleared her throat.

"Miss Covington!" he announced in a congenial tone. He folded the paper and tucked it into the side compartment on his leather briefcase before standing and offering his hand. "I apologize. It's so rare that I get a moment to relax and read the paper; I believe I was quite in another world."

"It's not a problem. I can only imagine how busy you are," Ariana said with a smile, shaking his hand. Then, suddenly, she remembered why she was here and how Briana Leigh would be expected to act. She rearranged her features into a pensive frown.

"Have a seat," Jessup said, gesturing at the chair next to his.

The puffed-up leather let out a quiet, comforting sigh as Ariana sat. Several legal documents were laid out across the table, each with bright pink tabs sticking out of their sides with the helpful words SIGN HERE in bold black letters.

"I'm so sorry for your loss," Jessup said, sitting next to her and rolling his chair closer to the table. He stopped messing with the mint, as if the occasion was too somber for such behavior.

"Thank you," Ariana said. Surreptitiously she eyed the paperwork, trying to discern any dollar amounts in all the legal gibberish. "Did you know my grandmother well?"

"Samantha Covington was a great lady. Not to mention one of our most important clients."

"She must be, if one of the firm's partners is flying out just to meet me," Ariana said, lifting one eyebrow.

Jessup cracked a smile. "We have four offices—Houston, St. Louis, Atlanta, and DC. There are about thirty other places I'm supposed to be right now, but I promised your grandmother I'd take care of her estate myself when the time came. I'm honored to be able to fulfill that promise."

"Thank you," Ariana said.

"This should be simple," Jessup said. "All you need to do is sign

where indicated, and then I'll be able to give you all the account numbers and keys."

He lifted an open box off the chair on his other side and placed
it on the table. Inside were several sets of keys, each with a white tag
hanging off of it, and a series of worn-looking bankbooks.

"Keys?" she asked.

"To the five safety deposit boxes containing all your mother and
grandmother's jewelry. To the ranch in Texas, the house in Florida,
the villa in Italy, the condo in Vail, the pied-à-terre in Paris. Also, the
cars," he said, lifting out one after the other. "You've got your Cadillac convertible, your grandmother's classic Benz, your father's Porsche,
and your mother's Infiniti. Your grandmother never had the heart to
sell those. The keys to the various vehicles at the other homes are all
with the caretakers, but I thought I'd bring these with me in case you
wanted me to have one of them shipped out."

Ariana's tongue was slick with saliva. She was actually about to
start drooling. Pied-à-terre in Paris? Villa in Italy? Condo in Vail? Her
choice of cars? Suddenly she wished she'd taken Lexa up on her offer
and brought her along, just so that she could have her pinch her.

"Miss Covington? Are you all right? Do you need some water?"
Mr. Jessup asked.

"Um, no, thank you. I'm fine," she said. She folded her hands
in her lap so he couldn't see them trembling, although he probably
would have thought she was overcome with stress rather than excitement. "Actually, you could have the Porsche shipped out, if you don't
mind taking care of that for me." She had detested Briana Leigh's

ridiculously ostentatious gold Cadillac. From everything she knew about Mr. Covington, she was sure his car was more classic—more understated.

"Of course not," Mr. Jessup said, making a quick note. Then he took out a second pen, uncapped it, and handed it to her. "All right, then. If you'll just show me your ID, we can get started."

Ariana's blood froze. "My ID?"

Did he think she wasn't who she said she was? Did he think she was some kind of fraud? She'd been living as Briana Leigh Covington for the past four months. And he had no idea the torture she'd had to live through before taking the name, just to secure it. How dare he ask for ID? Her fingers clenched the pen so hard the tips began to turn white under her fingernails.

"Yes, it's just a matter of course," Mr. Jessup said. "Legalities and all that. You do have it with you?"

Ariana breathed in deeply through her nose, telling herself to be patient. The man was just doing his job. He wasn't trying to out her. Slowly, concentrating on every move—on making them look casual— Ariana placed the pen down, reached into her bag and extracted her wallet. Her fingers were slick with sweat, so it took several frustrating tries to remove the license from its transparent casing. Mr. Jessup chuckled at her many attempts, which made her skin prickle. Then, finally, it slipped free. She handed it to him, held her breath, and waited.

The man barely glanced at it. "Thank you," he said, handing it back to her.

Ariana tucked the license away as her skin gradually returned to a normal temperature. It was fine. Everything was fine.

"Sign here," Jessup said, turning the first page toward her.

At first, Ariana's fingers were trembling so badly, she could hardly write Briana Leigh's name. But with each successive signature, her writing became more clear, more sure. She was worth millions. She had properties all over the world at her disposal. And within days, she'd have a car on campus. This was the single best day of her life.

"And here . . . ," Jessup said, putting the last piece of paper in front of her.

Ariana signed quickly, then clasped the pen in both hands over her heart, biting down on her lip in excitement. Slowly, Mr. Jessup slid the box toward her.

"All of your parents' accounts are electronic, so I've brought you the passwords and account numbers. But your grandmother was old school. She liked to write everything down herself," Mr. Jessup said fondly. "I thought you might want to have her records."

"Thank you," Ariana said, reaching for the first account book.

She tried not to be too quick about it, lest she appear greedy and not properly mournful, but she did have to look. She simply had to. She opened the account to its last entry and stared at the balance. It read $756,905.32.

"That's just her checkbook," Mr. Jessup said, almost apologetically. "The savings accounts, of course, are far more substantial."

Ariana felt suddenly faint. Her mouth went dry, and she shakily placed the book down on the table. She was rich. Filthy, stinking, disgustingly rich. She could take this checkbook right now, walk out of here, and buy herself *ten* cars if she wanted to. Or a few boats. Or a freaking town house on Capitol Hill.

"I think I'll take that water now, please," she said.

"Of course."

Mr. Jessup leaned forward and hit a button on a keypad at the center of the table. It let out a buzz. "Yes, Mr. Jessup?" a voice chirped.

"Miss Covington is in need of some water, please, Cheryl," he said.

"Right away, sir."

Ariana cleared her throat, gripping the arms on her chair. She had to calm down. She had to stop freaking out and think clearly. What would Briana Leigh do right now? Her grandmother had just died. What would she say?

"What about a funeral?" Ariana blurted suddenly.

"Oh, there will be no funeral," Mr. Jessup said. "Your grandmother wanted everything to be very low-key. She's being cremated this morning, and her ashes will be scattered at the ranch. Of course, you're more than welcome to come home and do that yourself if—"

"No," Ariana said, as cool, comforting relief coursed through her veins and filled her lungs. "That's okay. I . . . I don't think I could handle that."

Mr. Jessup smiled sympathetically. "I understand."

The assistant walked in and placed a clear glass of water in front of Ariana. She grabbed it and took a ladylike sip. Then another. Then another. The whole while, she stared at the other three account books in the box, barely able to stop herself from tearing into them.

"Well, I suppose our business is done here," Mr. Jessup said. He stood up and slipped a business card out of the inner pocket on his suit jacket and handed it to her. "Please feel free to call me if you have any questions."

"Of course," Ariana said, standing as well.

She barely looked at the card as she tucked it into her purse. Her mind was already rushing ahead to the insane shopping spree she was about to treat herself to. If only she were in New York instead of DC. But she could go there whenever she wanted to. Now she could even go to Paris to shop. She had a place to stay, all her own. Suddenly Ariana wondered what the apartment looked like. Maybe she'd spend the summer in Paris and have it redecorated. She could hire the finest designers in Europe and have furniture flown in from Italy and Spain and—

"It was very nice meeting you. I only wish it could have been under other circumstances," Mr. Jessup said, offering his hand again as he slipped his briefcase off the table.

"Nice to meet you, t—"

Ariana's voice died in her throat. Her eyes had just fallen on the top half of the folded newspaper sticking out of Mr. Jessup's bag. Instantly, her vision clouded over and her head went light. She grabbed the back of her chair to keep from going down. She'd lived through these episodes before, but never had one come on so fast. Never so unexpectedly. Alarmed, Ariana clung to the chair for dear life and gasped, feeling as if she was about to drown.

It couldn't be. It just couldn't be.

"Miss Covington?" Mr. Jessup's hand was on her arm. "Miss Covington, are you all right?"

*Breathe, Ariana. Just breathe.*

*In, one . . . two . . . three . . .*

*Out, one . . . two . . . three . . .*

*In, one . . . two . . . three . . .*

*Out, one . . . two . . . three . . .*

*In, one . . . two . . . three . . .*

*Out, one . . . two . . . three . . .*

"Here. Have some more water," Mr. Jessup was saying.

Ariana sat down hard in her chair and closed her eyes. Mr. Jessup pressed the water glass into her hand, but she couldn't find the power to move it to her mouth. She rocked back and forward, back and forward, trying to wipe the image from her mind.

"Miss Covington? Please, drink." He sounded panicked, and somehow that brought Ariana back to herself. Just slightly.

She lifted the water to her lips and gulped it this time. She felt the cold liquid sluice down her throat, coating her stomach and cooling her insides, and concentrated on those sensations. When the glass was empty, she closed her eyes and drew in one, large breath.

"Are you okay?" Mr. Jessup asked again. "Should I call the paramedics?"

"I'm fine. I'm sorry. I think I just . . ." She pressed her eyes closed tightly, trying to keep herself from looking at the paper again. Trying to come up with a reasonable excuse for her odd behavior. "I just realized the reality of it all," she rambled. "I just can't believe this is happening."

And then she could no longer stop herself. She opened her eyes and looked right at the folded newspaper. Right at the brightly colored photo.

It was. It was. It was *her*. "Can I see that?" she blurted. "The newspaper?"

Mr. Jessup's brow knit deeply, clearly baffled.

"Sometimes it helps if I focus on something else for a minute," Ariana explained impatiently. Her fingers itched to snatch the page, so she lifted her butt from the chair and sat down on her hands.

"Of course." Mr. Jessup placed the paper on the table in front of her. Ariana released her hands and spread it out flat on the glass. Splashed across the sports page was a huge, full-color photo of a girl, chasing a soccer ball across a bright green field in a gray and blue Georgetown jersey. Ariana gritted her teeth as she read the caption.

*Georgetown freshman phenom Reed Brennan takes the ball upfield in the Hoyas' routing of William and Mary yesterday at North Kehoe Field.*

Ariana clenched her teeth. And clenched. And clenched. It was all she could do to keep from screaming and tearing her hair out.

Reed Brennan in the flesh. Reed Brennan happy and healthy and sane. Reed Brennan, a freshman in college, while Ariana was two years behind, stuck pretending to be a high school junior. While Ariana should have been two years ahead.

"Miss Covington?" Mr. Jessup said tentatively.

Ariana blinked. The image of Reed had disappeared inside her fist. She had crumpled the entire front page in her fingers without even realizing it.

Taking a deep breath, Ariana told herself to stop. Stop, stop, stop. Everything was on the line right here, right now. And she was not going to let Reed Brennan screw up her life. Not again. She slowly released the page. Her palm was red with perspiration and black with newsprint. Reed Brennan's pretty little face was now a smudge.

"I'm so sorry, Mr. Jessup," Ariana said, standing again. "I was just thinking about my grandmother and . . . I'm sorry about your paper."

"It's quite all right, Miss Covington," he said, patting her on the shoulder. He glanced forlornly at the crumbled page. "I was finished with that section anyway."

Ariana forced a smile.

"Good luck with everything, my dear," he said with a sympathetic smile. Then he gave her shoulder one last squeeze and walked out.

Ariana turned slowly toward the table. She smoothed out the page with both hands, folded it, and tucked it into her purse. Then she dumped the keys and bankbooks into her tote bag, and closed that as well, dropping the empty box onto the table. As she turned to walk out of the conference room, she felt a black slick of anger slip down her spine.

Five minutes ago she'd been happier than she'd ever been. Five minutes ago she'd been dreaming about her apartment in Paris, her shopping spree, her new car. But now all she could think about was Reed Brennan. Reed Brennan, who was enrolled at one of the best colleges in the country. A university that just happened to be ten miles from where Ariana was living.

This could not be happening. This simply could not be happening.

# NEAR MISS

There were twenty-four texts and voice mails on Ariana's cell phone as she stepped off the bus just outside the sprawling Georgetown campus. Texts from her friends, asking if she was okay, whether she was coming back for afternoon classes. A voice mail from Palmer suggesting they hang out tonight and lay low, telling her he'd fly back to Texas with her if she needed him to. Another from Jasper, just checking in. She listened to them without really hearing them, then turned her phone off as she stepped through the elaborate iron gates between the two brick gatehouses leading to the oldest part of campus.

Reed Brennan was here somewhere. Ariana could feel her.

She tucked her phone away and strode toward the circle at the center of the great lawn. All around her the stately gray buildings loomed, hidden eyes looking out at her, people watching from every angle. Was Reed one of them? Did she know Ariana was coming for her? Could she feel Ariana's presence, too?

A bicycler zipped by, chatting on his Bluetooth. A group of girls in T-shirts displaying sorority letters sipped coffees and gossiped on a nearby bench. Students hurried across the sunlit paths, huddled into their winter jackets, rushing off to their next class or to meet their professors or have lunch with friends.

And Reed Brennan was among them, somewhere.

Ariana's fingertips tingled as she straightened out her hands, then curled them into fists. She paused at the corner of two walkways and scanned the faces around her.

Reed Brennan did not deserve to be here. Did not deserve to be alive. After all the pain and misery and loss she'd caused. After all the awful things Ariana had been forced to do thanks to her. She did not deserve to exist.

What she did deserve was to feel pain. Excruciating, unbearable, merciless pain.

Which, luckily, Ariana Osgood knew how to inflict.

She took a step forward, ready for however long a search she'd need to conduct, when suddenly, just like that, she was there. Right there. Striding her long, confident, Reed Brennan strides toward the library, her thick brown hair swinging behind her in natural waves. Ariana's eyes narrowed. Her nostrils flared. She gripped her forearm with her hand and zeroed in.

Reed was a fast walker, but Ariana quickly closed the gap between the two of them, taking in Reed's expensive Chloé boots, her designer jeans, her cashmere jacket. Hating every detail of her, from her unpolished, short nails to her plain black headband. She was five feet away, then two, one. When Ariana's hand came down on her shoulder, she yelped and whirled around.

"Yes?" the girl snapped, hand to her heart. Her too-close-together eyes came even closer over her pointy nose.

Ariana blinked. It was not Reed at all.

"I . . . I'm sorry," Ariana stammered, feeling suddenly and supremely stupid. "I thought . . . I thought you were someone else."

The girl's face relaxed. "Oh. That's okay." She smiled and started to turn, but paused. "Actually . . . you do look kinda familiar. What's your name?"

Ariana swallowed hard. She had forgotten for a moment who she was. Who she needed to be to survive. Who she was now and must always be from now on. A girl who had never even met Reed Brennan—never even heard of her. A girl who had no idea of the destruction Reed Brennan had wrought.

She took a breath and smiled. It was a near miss, but that's all it had been. A miss. She couldn't start obsessing about Reed Brennan again. That course of action only ever led to bad things, horrible things. She had to stop this here and now before she completely lost control.

"I'm Briana Leigh Covington," she said firmly. "Of the Texas Covingtons."

The girl's brow knit. "Oh. Okay. Guess not, then."

As she turned around and headed into the library, Ariana did a 180 and walked back across campus, keeping her head down.

A near miss. That was all it was. But if Reed Brennan *had* seen her—if she had looked into the face of her enemy—it would all be over. Ariana could not allow herself to go down that path.

She had many, many other things to focus on. More important things, more positive things. Things like her new fortune, her perfect boyfriend, and the rest of her perfectly charmed life.

# CELEBRATION

The following morning dawned as bright and crisp as the day before, and Ariana was feeling much more herself as she walked across campus toward the dining hall. The white spire of the APH chapel seemed to smile down at her approvingly from above, and she realized for the first time how very at home she felt among the red brick buildings, the winding walkways, the stone arches of APH. She was up and out before everyone else on her floor, but that was the way she wanted it today. She wanted some time alone to breathe. Some time to focus on herself. Some time to just be here, to relish how far she'd come.

Some time to repeat to herself over and over again the grand total of what she was now worth, a number so very long she stumbled over it every time she tried to conjure it up. Just thinking of it now, Ariana giggled to herself and shivered inside her wool coat.

"Well, someone's happy this morning."

Ariana jumped as Jasper fell into step with her, his breath making a large cloud of steam in the morning air.

"What are you doing up so early?" Ariana asked.

"I'm a morning person," he said, tilting his head. "Actually, I'll admit it. I was waiting for you."

Ariana's heart skipped a beat. "So you're stalking me now?" she joked.

"Do you want me to stalk you?" Jasper joked back. But there was something hopeful behind the playful gleam in his eye—which Ariana chose to ignore. "Seriously, though. I just wanted to see how you were doing. About your grandmother."

*Fantastically, thanks,* Ariana thought. "I'm okay," she said in a melancholy tone.

"Well, if you need anything, I'm at your service," he told her, with a slight bow of his head, his blond bangs falling across one eye. "I know that between Palmer and Lexa you probably have all your bases covered, but the offer stands."

"Thank you," Ariana replied, touched.

Arriving at the dining hall, Jasper leaned back against the outer wall and looked up at the sun, letting out a contented sigh. His gold and blue tie was knotted tightly, unlike most of the boys who went for the more casual, open-necked, loosened-knot look.

"Don't you just wish we could stay out here all day?" he mused.

"On a day like this, yes," Ariana said with a smile.

Jasper tugged an orange pill bottle out of his pocket and popped it open.

"What are you taking?" Ariana knit her brow as she tilted her head to see the label. The prescription was issued by a Dr. Lance Montgomery. "Do you have a doctor in the family?" she asked, intrigued.

"Nosy much?" Jasper teased. He tossed the pill in his mouth and swallowed it dry, then nodded casually in greeting to a pair of teachers who walked by them and into the building. "Yes, my cousin is a general practitioner, and he writes my allergy prescriptions for me."

"That's convenient," Ariana said.

"Beats having to find a local doctor who isn't a complete buffoon," Jasper said. As he tucked the bottle away, his cell phone beeped. He yanked it out of the side pocket on his messenger bag and rolled his eyes at the screen.

"My mother again," he groused. "No, Mom, I do not know whether the sheets at the Ritz frickin' Carlton are Egyptian cotton or not!" He yelled into the phone, which was, of course, not connected to anything. He sighed and shoved it away again. Ariana laughed.

"Your mother definitely sounds like a woman who knows what she wants," she said as she hugged her chemistry book to her chest.

"Yes, she is," Jasper said. He shook his head in an exasperated but fond way. "Do you want to meet my parents this weekend, Miss Covington?" He asked, pushing himself away from the wall. "Because I'd love to introduce them to you."

"Depends," she said, lifting a shoulder. She looked up at him through her thick lashes. "Will I like them?"

Jasper grinned. "Most girls worry about whether the parents will like *them*."

Ariana turned and opened the door to the dining hall. With one hand on the handle, she leaned toward him, her coat just brushing his.

"First of all, your parents are not *the* parents to me. Palmer's parents are," Ariana teased. His face fell slightly, but then he tossed his head, flicking his bangs away from his eyes and coming back to himself. "And secondly," Ariana said, smiling, "I'm not most girls."

Slowly, Jasper smiled back. Ariana walked into the dining hall ahead of him, and just before the door closed in his face, she heard him say under his breath, "No, you're not."

# SEVENTY-FIVE PERCENT

"See, the problem with the Stone and Grave Ball is that you have to take a member of Stone and Grave," Maria said, lazily turning the page of last year's Atherton-Pryce Hall *Golden,* the slim hardcover yearbook. She was lying on her stomach on the floor of her and Lexa's room in a tank top and pajama pants, a bottle of sparkling water within reach. "It cuts down your potential dates by about seventy-five percent."

"Ah, Maria. She can only do the heavy math if the topic is boys or sales," Lexa joked, leaning back on her pillows. She opened a *Vogue* magazine and started to page through it.

Ariana laughed as she and Soomie leaned in toward the yearbook on either side of Maria. "What about Carlton Goff?" Ariana suggested, looking over Maria's ponytail at Soomie. In his picture from the year prior, Carlton's now short hair was long around the ears, and he wore a serious expression. "He's kinda cute."

"Ugh. Have you ever actually spoken to Carlton Goff?" Soomie asked.

Ariana shook her head. "Not really."

Soomie leaned back on her hands, her long black hair dangling almost to the floor. "That boy is (A) condescending, (B) nasal, and (C) needs to buy stock in Listerine."

"So true," Lexa confirmed with a wrinkle of her nose. She flipped a page and held up the perfume sample she found there for a sniff.

"Ew. Then why did he get into Stone and Grave?" Ariana asked, reaching for her own bottle of water.

"Legacy," the other three girls answered in unison.

"Ah," Ariana replied knowingly.

"Well, there has to be somebody in here Soomie can ask," Maria said, flipping to the next page.

"Why are we all focused on Soomie, anyway? Don't you need a date too, Maria?" Lexa said, sitting up. She had torn out the perfume sample and was now swiping the scent strip across her wrists. "No offense," she added, nudging Soomie's back with her bare toe.

"None taken," Soomie replied.

Lexa and Soomie eyed Maria with interest as Ariana casually looked away, suddenly riveted by the pilling atop her cashmere sock. Maria blithely flipped another page, lifting her tiny shoulders. "I don't mind being dateless. Soomie, however, does."

Ariana looked up in time to see Lexa and Soomie exchange a glance.

"I've got it! What about one of the newbies," Maria said, sitting up straight and swinging her legs around in front of her. "You can ask Adam! Or Jasper!"

Ariana's heart twisted in an odd way at the mention of Jasper. She tugged the now abandoned yearbook onto her thighs and flipped to last year's juniors.

"Or Landon," Lexa put in.

There was a brief pause. "I'm so over Landon," Soomie replied. "And Adam . . . I don't know. He and Brigit were really close. I'd just feel weird. But Jasper . . . I've actually had some moments with him."

"*Real*-ly?" Lexa asked, sliding off the bed and onto the floor with the rest of them. "What kind of moments?"

Soomie blushed. "I don't know. I think he might like me."

"Do you?" Ariana asked. Her voice sounded tense. But why? She shook out her arms, trying to relax. It would be great if Jasper liked Soomie. Right?

"Why didn't you mention this *before* we spent half an hour going through the yearbook?" Maria asked, taking a swig of her water.

"I don't know," Soomie said, blushing even darker and flipping her hair. "But he's always making excuses to talk to me. Like asking for my help with trig and checking to see if I need refills at lunch."

*That's just because he's lazy and a gentleman,* Ariana thought.

She found herself squeezing her water bottle and placed it back down on the floor. She stared down at her wet, cold fingers as Lexa and Maria peppered Soomie with questions about her and Jasper's potential. Her face felt hot, and she realized, suddenly, that she had thought that Jasper liked *her*. Not that she would ever do anything about it. It was just kind of nice to feel special. But if he'd been treating Soomie the same way all along . . . then she wasn't special at all.

*But you're special to Palmer. That's all that matters,* she told herself, feeling silly and more than a little bit selfish.

"You guys seem to hang out a lot, Ana," Soomie said suddenly. "Has he ever mentioned me?"

Ariana bit her lip. "No, actually, he hasn't."

"Oh." Soomie looked down at her lap.

"But that doesn't mean anything," Ariana said in a rush. "He's a guy."

The other girls looked at one another knowingly. That argument explained away all manners of behavior.

"Well, do you think you could talk to him?" Maria asked. "At least find out if he has a date yet. Then we'll know if Soomie should even bother."

Ariana swallowed hard. "Sure. I'll talk to him."

"Really? Oh, thank you, thank you, thank you!" Soomie said, flinging her arms around Ariana's neck. "You're the best, Ana."

Ariana smiled as she hugged Soomie back. Somehow she couldn't exactly see Soomie and Jasper as a couple, but if this was what her friend wanted, of course she would try to help her. No matter how bad an idea she thought it was.

# TRUTH

"So, you're doing okay?" Palmer asked Ariana on Wednesday evening, as they kicked back in what was now becoming their spot at the Hill. It was the comfiest suede couch with the best view of the river, so of course it belonged to the most admired couple in the school. Ariana cuddled into Palmer's shoulder and slipped her arm around his waist, relishing the feel of his six-pack under his shirt.

"Oh, I'm doing just fine," she murmured.

Palmer ran his fingers over the hair on the crown of her head, lifting it and dropping it over and over in a rhythmic way. He kissed her part, then rested his chin on top of her head.

"Are you sure? You're not upset that you're not going to have a chance to say good-bye?"

Ariana cringed. Right. He was talking about Grandma Covington. Why did she keep forgetting about that? It was kind of an important detail of Briana Leigh's life.

"I've said good-bye in my own way," she told him, infusing her voice with melancholy. "She didn't want me to have to go to all the trouble of traveling home. That's how she was. She always put me first."

Ariana made all of this up off the cuff. If anything, in the brief time she'd seen Briana Leigh and her grandmother together, Grandma Covington couldn't have cared less about what made Briana Leigh happy or comfortable. In that relationship, it was Grandma's way or the highway, which was exactly how Briana Leigh had ended up on a plane to Atherton-Pryce against her will. But Palmer didn't need to know that.

"Hey, guys! What's going on?" Micah Granger said, lifting a hand as he passed by with some of his friends.

"Yo, Palmer!" Rob Mellon added, striding by with his arm around Tahira. "Halo in my room later. Time for me to whoop your ass."

"Yeah, yeah. We'll see," Palmer replied.

Tahira gave Ariana a wave as the couple headed out through the double door. Then a pack of junior girls walked in, glancing covetously at Palmer and giggling on their way to the coffee counter. Ariana smirked and cuddled closer to her man. This was where she was supposed to be. Palmer was the most popular guy on campus. Everyone adored him. All the guys wanted to be him, and now all the girls wanted to be her just because she was with him.

Ariana followed the girls with her eyes on their way to the coffee counter, just to make sure they knew she was not intimidated. But when she caught sight of Jasper standing on line, she flinched. He leaned back against the pastry case, his legs crossed at the ankle, and simply stared at her. He didn't blink or look away when she caught his eye.

Even though Ariana detested being the first to break eye contact, she did. She turned her face toward Palmer's chest and cuddled closer to him. She had no idea what Jasper was thinking, but she felt the need to let him know—right then and there—that Palmer was the guy she wanted. That this was the life she wanted. The life she had been working toward all these months as Briana Leigh Covington. And even all those years she'd lived as Ariana Osgood.

"Okay, what's up with Lexa?" Palmer said suddenly.

Ariana's heart dropped. She looked at the other side of the room, where she knew Lexa, Maria, and Soomie were sitting with a few of their sophomore hangers-on—Quinn as well as Jessica and Melanie. She watched as Lexa crumbled a disinfecting wipe, then snatched another from Quinn, who was holding it out to her. She scrubbed at her hands maniacally, as if she was trying to remove a permanent pen mark from her skin. Maria and Soomie were both eyeing her, clearly disturbed.

"What do you mean?" Ariana asked blithely, as if she saw nothing wrong, even though the pit of her stomach was turning inside out.

"She's been acting kind of weird lately," Palmer said, sitting up straight so that Ariana had to sit up, too. She picked up her coffee and took a sip, keeping an eye on Lexa. "I mean, that's the fourth time I've seen her washing her hands today."

Ariana gulped. "Really?" She grabbed a napkin from the table and touched it to her lips. "I don't know. Hasn't she always been a little bit cleanly? I mean her room is so organized, it's like she's practically OCD."

"Maybe a little, but this is weird," Palmer said. His expression hovered somewhere between disgusted and concerned as he watched his ex-girlfriend toss the wipe aside and snag yet another. "I don't know, do you think that maybe this rift between her parents is affecting her more than she's let on?"

"Well, she is an only child," Ariana replied. "It's hard for only children when they start to see their family break up."

"I guess."

Across the room, Soomie leaned forward and took the wipe out of Lexa's hand before she could remove another layer of skin. Lexa blinked and looked up, as if startled. Soomie placed her hands over Lexa's and said a few words, and Lexa seemed to realize, for the first time, what she'd been doing. She slumped back into the couch as if exhausted, and stared down at her hands, which were raw, red, and trembling.

Ariana's breath started to come quick and shallow. She had to get Lexa back on an even keel. If she didn't, the results could be disastrous. For both of them.

"I've been thinking, maybe you, me, Lexa, and Connie should go out on a double date," Ariana said, turning toward Palmer, suddenly bright-eyed.

His brows shot up. "You think?"

"Yeah. Why not? It could be fun," Ariana said, turning her knees toward his.

"Fun. To go on a date with my current girlfriend, my ex-girlfriend, and her current boyfriend," Palmer deadpanned.

Ariana took a breath for patience. "I know it could be weird, but she's my best friend, and you and Conrad are friends too. Sooner or later we're all going to have to hang out together. The sooner it happens, the sooner we can get past the uncomfortable part and start feeling okay about the whole thing."

Palmer frowned, considering this, and took a long sip of his coffee. "Okay," he said finally. "If it's something you think we should do, I'm in. But let's do it after parents' weekend. Things are going to be insane for the next few days."

"Thank you!" Ariana planted a kiss on his cheek and leaned back into him again. All she had to do was show Lexa some actual fun. Distract her with total normalcy. Make her understand that life could, in fact, go on exactly as it had been before, even after what had happened with Kaitlynn.

It was a truth Ariana lived every single day of her life. If Lexa was smart, she'd figure out how to live it too.

# NOT A CARE

"All I know is, these bags are *not* going to fit in that car," Soomie said, dropping her many paper shopping bags as she sat in a small Georgetown café on Thursday evening. "But I do so love that car," she added, looking longingly out the window at Ariana's gunmetal gray, classic Porsche 944 convertible, which had just been delivered that morning. It was parked out on the street below the flattering glow of a streetlight, and two college guys in backward baseball caps were just now stopping to admire it.

"Don't you, though?" Ariana asked giddily.

When Maria had floated the idea of a Stone and Grave Ball–related shopping jaunt, Ariana had jumped at the chance to drive her friends to the chic merchants' district in her new ride. Of course, the "backseat" was the size of a bread box, but it did come equipped with seat belts, so Maria and Soomie and crowded in, letting Lexa take the front. Everyone had enjoyed the drive, even Lexa, who hadn't whipped out a single disinfectant wipe all afternoon. Still, Ariana sighed as she looked around at the four girls' many purchases. Soomie was right. They couldn't have fit this haul in the back of a Hummer.

"No worries," Lexa said, slipping her phone from her purse. "I'll just have Keiko call one of Daddy's drivers and have him come pick it all up."

Ariana grinned. Not only was Lexa with it today, she was even being proactive. Plus she had purchased a gorgeous black Marchesa gown for the ball, gabbing on about how Conrad loved her in black. Maybe Palmer was wrong. Maybe Lexa was simply going through a cleanly phase. Leaning back in her chair, Ariana decided to savor the moment. She was off campus, relaxing with her friends, and didn't have a care in the world. She could have sat in that café all night long and been perfectly content.

"Hello, ladies," a tall, blond waiter appeared at their table, pad and pen at the ready. "Can I take your order?"

"We'll all have oriental chicken salad, low-fat dressing, and no nuts," Maria said, handing him the menus. "And we'll stick with water," she added, gesturing at the four filled glasses on the table.

"Hey! I was going to get pasta," Ariana said, grabbing in vain for her menu.

"Not if you intend to be bloat-free for the ball, you're not," Maria replied.

"Maria, please," Lexa said, turning off her phone after her brief call. "Do not try to foist your eating disorder off on the rest of us."

Maria rolled her eyes and slumped back in her chair. "I'll have a turkey burger and fries," Lexa told the waiter.

"Ooh, me too!" Ariana said.

"I'll stick with the salad," Soomie told him.

"Okay. Let me know if you need anything else, ladies," the waiter said with a grin. Soomie eyed him from behind as he turned and pushed through the doors to the kitchen.

"Checking out the merchandise, Soom?" Maria joked.

"I don't think he's on the menu," Ariana added, earning a laugh from her friends.

Soomie blushed as she turned around again. She checked her BlackBerry quickly, then placed it next to her silverware on the table. With both hands she smoothed her already sleek black hair, then cleared her throat.

"He kind of looks like Jasper, don't you think?" she said, ducking her chin toward the table with a giddy smile.

Ariana's stomach twisted tightly. She toyed with her water glass, spinning it in a circle, and tried to look casual. She knew what was coming next.

"Have you had a chance to talk to him yet?" Soomie asked.

"Not yet," Ariana said, wincing.

Soomie's face fell, and she sat back hard in her chair. "Oh."

"I'm sorry, Soomie. It's just been a crazy few days with my grand-mother and dealing with the car delivery people this morning and every-thing," Ariana said in a rush. "I feel like I've barely even been in class."

"It's okay," Soomie said. "It's just . . . the ball is next weekend."

"I know," Ariana said, guilt weighing down on her shoulders. "I'm sorry. I'll talk to him, I promise."

As the other girls turned the conversation back to their many purchases, Ariana leaned back in her chair and sipped her water, trying to figure out why, exactly, she was so hesitant to talk to Jasper for Soomie. She didn't begrudge Soomie a boyfriend. It was just . . . if Jasper started going out with one of her best friends, the casual flirting would stop. It would have to. Which would kind of suck.

*Stop it, Ariana. You can't keep all the boys for yourself,* she told herself, shaking her head slightly.

The bell over the door pinged, and Ariana automatically looked up. Walking through the door were three girls in Georgetown windbreakers, their hair back in sporty ponytails. For a whole ten seconds Ariana's heart stopped. Stopped until she could see the face on the third girl, which was blocked by her friends. Finally, one of them laughed, turning to the side to whack her friend on the arm, and the third girl was revealed.

Revealed to *not* be Reed Brennan.

Ariana breathed in, long and slow.

"Maybe I should ask him to be my date for the ball," Soomie was saying, when Ariana tuned in again. "Not that we *need* dates, but still—"

And just like that, Ariana couldn't wait to get the hell out of the café.

Maybe she wasn't a linger-all-night type of girl after all.

# CRISIS AVERTED

For the welcoming dinner that Friday night, the vast ballroom in Pryce Hall was tastefully decorated with floral arrangements in autumn colors, and a welcome banner was strung across the widest part of the room, reading simply, WELCOME, PARENTS! in silver glitter. A string quartet played in the corner farthest from the tables, and waiters in shirts and ties circulated the room, offering traditional hors d'oeuvres like salmon en croute and mini spring rolls. Ariana sighed, her arms folded behind her blue wrap dress as she attempted to focus on the conversation between Palmer's mother and Lexa's father. But she was too busy wondering why Lexa was so late. Earlier that afternoon she'd told Ariana she had an errand to run and would meet them here at seven, but it was now almost eight o'clock.

Just to make matters worse, the subject of the conversation couldn't have been more boring. If Ariana heard the words "filibuster" or "amendment" one more time, she was going to start yawning unattractively. In fact, across the circle, Maria was doing just that as Soomie checked her watch. Both their parents were late.

"Sorry," Palmer whispered in her ear, touching his fingertips to the small of her back in a very pleasant way. "Sometimes these two get carried away, being from opposite sides of the aisle and all."

"It's okay," Ariana whispered back with a smile. He looked incredibly handsome in his gray suit and blue tie, much like a young senator himself. "Keep your hand there and all is forgiven."

Palmer grinned and moved his hand up and down her back in a soothing circle. Ariana stepped a bit closer to him, relishing the fact that he was displaying their relationship so boldly in front of both his parents and Lexa's. At least something good was coming out of this yawn-fest of a gathering.

A burst of sudden, raucous laughter nearly knocked Ariana over in her new Louboutins. She turned and glanced over her shoulder. Standing near the wall under the glittering banner was Jasper, who was doubled over laughing with his hand on the shoulder of an older man, clearly his father. The man was rotund and balding, but perfectly coiffed in a dark suit and red tie. He looked exactly as Jasper would have looked if someone had hooked up an air pump to him and gone to work. Standing near the wall on Jasper's other side, talking quietly with a few suited ladies, was a diminutive woman with blonde curls, an angular face, and a sharp eye. Clearly, Jasper's mother.

Jasper's dad cracked another joke, and the growing crowd around him burst out in another round of laughter. Mr. Montgomery reminded her of her own dad, who was always the center of attention at any gathering.

Suddenly Jasper looked up and caught her staring. He smirked and lifted his glass, and Ariana snapped her head around to face forward, her cheeks red with embarrassment.

*What is* wrong *with me?* she berated herself. *Palmer. Focus on Palmer.*

"Lexa! There you are!" Mrs. Greene said suddenly.

Everyone in the little group turned. Lexa paused and slowly faced them, her eyes narrowed as if she didn't recognize her own mother.

"Oh. Hi," she said.

Lexa looked slightly unkempt in her black pencil skirt and wrinkled white top. Her skin was waxy, and although she'd applied eyeliner, she'd spaced on the mascara, which gave her a sort of frightened aspect. Her ankle wobbled as she stepped toward them. Ariana saw Mr. and Mrs. Liriano exchange an alarmed glance. She knew the feeling. What was up with Lexa now?

"Where have you been?" Her mother looked her up and down in a disapproving way as Lexa planted a perfunctory kiss on her cheek.

"Mother. Father," Lexa said flatly, ignoring the question. "Hey, guys," she said to her friends. "Hello, Lirianos." She lifted a hand half-heartedly.

Lexa grabbed a flute of champagne from the tray of a passing waiter. "I've got kind of a lot going on right now."

She sipped the champagne and tapped her foot as if nervous, not looking anyone in the eye.

"Lexa!" Her mother whipped the glass out of her hand. "No drinking!"

"Mom!" Lexa whined, her shoulders slumping.

Ariana and Palmer exchanged a glance as Mr. Liriano cleared his throat and looked away. Maria and Soomie leaned toward one another, whispering under their breath as if they were trying to come up with a plan to help, but no one knew what to do, what with all the adults hovering around.

"Lexa. What has gotten into you?" Senator Greene said, his voice a low rumble.

Lexa opened her mouth to answer, but Ariana placed her hand on Lexa's wrist to stop her.

"We've all been under a lot of stress lately with the SATs coming up and finals," Ariana said, smiling at the adults. "Honestly, Lexa just hasn't been getting much sleep."

Instantly, Lexa's mother's face was lined with concern. She handed both her champagne flute and Lexa's to Maria and Soomie. They took them, obviously startled at being suddenly treated like the help. Mrs. Greene stepped toward her daughter.

"Is that true, honey? You haven't been sleeping?" she said, cupping Lexa's face with both hands.

Lexa's cast her eyes down and nodded.

"You know how you get when you're overtired," her mother said as she wrapped one arm around Lexa to face the group.

"I'm the same way, Lexa," Palmer's father said in his congenial way. "I'm a bear when I don't get my eight hours."

"It's true. He could never do my job," Congresswoman Liriano joked. The others, including Ariana, laughed half-heartedly.

"What're we going to do with you?" Mrs. Greene asked, shaking her head at her daughter.

"Don't worry, Mrs. Greene," Ariana said, reaching for Lexa's hand. "I'll make sure she takes care of herself from now on."

She gave Lexa's fingers an extra-hard squeeze, driving her point home.

"Well, thank you, Briana Leigh," Mrs. Greene said. "It's nice to know that Lexa has an old friend here, looking out for her."

Ariana beamed with pride over Mrs. Greene's approval.

"Lacey, there are the Janikowskis," Senator Greene said suddenly. "We must go talk to them before they leave for Greece."

"All right," Lexa's mother said. She shot an apologetic look at the group. "Duty calls." Then she turned to Ariana and took her free hand. "I'm looking forward to talking to you more at our brunch tomorrow, Briana Leigh." She kissed Lexa on the forehead. "Get some sleep tonight, honey, okay?"

"Okay, Mom," Lexa said quietly.

As Mr. and Mrs. Greene sauntered off, Ariana sighed with relief at another crises averted. It was time for her to focus on keeping Lexa in check, before the girl completely lost it and did something both of them would regret.

# BREAKDOWN

"Everyone ready?" April Coorigan asked late Friday night as she walked along the end of the long line of Stone and Grave members.

"Ready," Ariana replied.

"*So* ready," Tahira put in, lifting her hood over her head.

The double doors at the front of the line opened, and the brotherhood began to walk inside slowly, heads bowed. Ariana lifted her own hood and bowed her head. For the last hour, April and Connie had gone over the meeting ritual with the five new members of Stone and Grave so that they would be ready for their first official gathering as brother and sisters. Ariana's steps were light as she entered the circular stone room where she had been locked inside the coffin with Jasper. This was it. This was the moment she'd been waiting for, ever since Lexa had first spilled about the secret society.

Slowly, Lexa led the group around the open graves. All along the stone walls, candles of various shapes and sizes flickered. Around the open graves, dozens of skulls had been placed, just like the ones Ariana had seen on the night she and the other potential members had first been introduced to Stone and Grave a couple of months back. That night seemed like it had happened a million years ago. Not only had Brigit still been alive, but Kaitlynn had been there as well. And because of Kaitlynn, Ariana had been full of anger and fear, unable to fully focus on the opportunity being laid out before her. But now all of that was over. Blissfully, mercifully over. And now she was here. Right where she was supposed to be.

Lexa stopped near the top of the room, right behind the gravestone that read Becky Sharp. Palmer stopped next to her, behind the Starbuck stone. Conrad was next in line as Lear, then April as Miss Temple, then Soomie, Rob, and so on, standing in order of their rank in the society. For a moment, Ariana felt a twinge over being near the end of the line, but at least she wasn't last. That spot belonged to Jasper, being that he was last alphabetically in their pledge class. Tahira stood behind her Sister Carrie headstone, and then Ariana took her place, glancing down to admire the name Portia, which was stamped onto hers in big, bold letters. Behind her, Landon took his spot as Pip—a name that made Ariana wonder if the Stone and Grave membership knew about him and Maria after all, since Maria was Estella. Then Adam stood behind Oliver Twist, and finally, Jasper took his place as Amory Blaine.

Christian Thacker stepped forward and closed the doors, then returned to his place in the circle. Lexa lifted her head and removed her hood.

"We are the Stone and Grave," she said loudly, firmly.

"We are the Stone and Grave," Ariana and the rest of the brotherhood repeated as one.

Lexa stepped forward, carefully skirting her headstone, breaking the circle. "Welcome to our new members!" she said with a smile.

The room burst out in applause and shouts. Ariana and the other new members laughed happily. She caught Palmer's eye from across the room and felt his pride radiating through her. Her next instinct was to look at Jasper, but she refused. He was her friend, and he was going to be with Soomie—at least maybe he was—if she ever got around to talking to him about her.

"You may all be seated," Lexa said, removing her hood from her hair.

Everyone tucked their black robes beneath them and hit the floor. Ariana hesitated only a split second, wondering why a room full of millionaires couldn't afford chairs, but then she sat. The robe was thick and kept the cold of the concrete from seeping through to her skin, and as she brought it over her knees, tucking it around her shins like a blanket, she was just grateful it wasn't a burlap sack. She nudged her hood off her head, following the brotherhood's lead, and smiled.

"Our first order of business is the Stone and Grave Ball next weekend," Lexa began, her voice as clear as a bell, ringing out across the large room. "I understand a few of you have yet to RSVP. Manners, people. We don't want to look bad in comparison to the other chapters. Let's get those cards returned so that our hosts can have time to prepare."

A murmur went through the room as April and Soomie eyed everyone suspiciously. Ariana almost laughed. Those two *would* take other people's lack of organizational skills as a personal affront. Then Soomie's eyes fell on Jasper, and she blushed and looked down at her lap. Ariana leaned forward to look at Jasper. He was smirking in Soomie's direction. And was he also . . . blushing? Had she already asked him to the ball without telling Ariana?

Ariana's heart flew to her throat, and her fingers curled into the folds of her robe. She took a deep breath and forced her fists to open again.

*That would be a good thing,* she reminded herself. *A very good thing.*

But it wasn't. She had thought that Jasper liked her. Whether or not she liked him back was irrelevant. It was like Thomas and Reed all over again, watching the two of them make gooey eyes at each other when he was supposed to belong to her. What the hell was going on here? Why was this always happening to her?

"Is it just me or is your butt freezing?" Tahira whispered, leaning toward her.

Ariana flinched. Suddenly the room came into focus. She took a deep breath and looked at Soomie again. It was just Soomie. Innocent little Soomie. And all her attention was focused on Lexa. Ariana uncurled her fingers, which had tightened again into fists.

*Control, Ariana. Get control. It's not like she's making a play for your boyfriend. Jasper is just a friend.*

"We also have a bit of business to complete concerning the new members," Lexa said. April reached behind her and lifted a black folder off the floor to hand to Lexa. "Each of you will have to sign this confidentiality agreement," Lexa said, opening the folder. She lifted the pages inside, one by one, checking them over. "We've already got one typed up for each of you so you'll just have to—"

Suddenly Lexa froze. Everyone sat and waited for her to continue. And waited. And waited. But she simply sat there, some of the papers in her hand, the folder open on her lap, staring down.

"Sister Becky Sharp?" Palmer said finally, gently.

"Why is this in here?" Lexa's voice was shrill in the silence. Shrill and loud. She dropped the papers in her hand and picked up the offending page. "*Why* is this in here? Is this some kind of joke, April? Some kind of sick joke?"

"It's Miss Temple," April said calmly. "And I don't know what you're talking about."

Lexa got up, scattering the papers and the folder everywhere, and shoved the page into April's face. "I'm talking about *this*. What is *this* doing in the folder? Are you just that stupid, or did you leave it there on purpose? Because last I checked, *Miss Temple,* Lillian Oswald is no longer with us!"

A wave of total dizziness and nausea crashed over Ariana. *No longer with us.* Did she really have to say it that way?

Conrad got up and put his large hand on Lexa's back. "It was just a simple mistake, Becky," he said in a soothing tone. "Give it to me. We'll just burn it."

"No!" Lexa shouted, whirling on him. "It's not a simple mistake! It's not! Things have to be done a certain way around here. They have to be *done.* Done. Done the way they're supposed to be done. Not this way. This is not the way this is supposed to happen, do you understand? I try! I try to make everything perfect! I can't keep having these things go wrong! I can't! I can't have this on my hands! I can't have this on my hands!"

*On her hands,* Ariana thought with a sinking realization. This was why Lexa kept washing her hands, carrying disinfecting wipes everywhere. She was trying to clean off the blood. The blood she imagined she had on her hands.

Everyone in the room was starting to mumble and shift uncomfortably as Lexa completely broke down in front of them. Ariana knew what was coming. Any second Lexa was going to go there. She was going to say something about the murder. About the blood. It was right there on the tip of her tongue. Terror seized Ariana's heart like an ice-cold vise grip.

"Can't have what on your hands, babe?" Conrad said, completely breaking Stone and Grave protocol. "What are you talking about?"

Lexa's eyes were desperate as she opened her mouth to speak. Desperately searching for a lifeline. For someone to help her.

"Conrad, I—"

Without a moment to rethink it, Ariana hurtled herself to her feet. "Lexa!"

Every single person in the room turned to look at Ariana. Lexa's eyes flicked past Conrad's shoulder and widened when they came to rest on Ariana's panicked face. And then she looked down at the floor.

"I'm sorry. I can't do this," Lexa said. "I have to go."

Then she dropped Lillian's form on the floor and ran out, letting the doors slam behind her.

"What was *that* about?" Rob said.

Instantly, everyone started talking. Tahira got up and nudged Ariana. "What the hell was that? Why did you yell at her?"

"I . . . I wanted to make sure she was okay," Ariana said off the cuff. Her fear was already beginning to subside, leaving behind the clarity of what she had just done. The oddity of her actions. "Was I that loud? I didn't realize."

Tahira simply shrugged, watching the mayhem as the meeting deteriorated around them.

"Maybe I should go after her," Ariana said.

"No."

Palmer's voice filled the room. He was right at her shoulder. A chill went down her spine as his directive brought all conversation to a halt.

"No one goes anywhere," Palmer said. He squeezed Ariana's hand, then turned to the circle. "I want to see the execs right now. The rest of you hang out until we've had a chance to talk."

Palmer planted a comforting kiss on Ariana's temple, then walked over to an indentation in the wall, just behind Lexa's headstone. Conrad, April, Soomie, and Rob followed. Ariana watched them closely. She knew they had to be discussing Lexa, and she had to find out what they were saying.

"Hey," Jasper said, appearing at her left shoulder. "Anyone ever tell you you look hot in that robe?"

Ariana narrowed her eyes at him. "Don't you mean Soomie looks hot?" she said.

Then, leaving him with his mouth gaping open, she walked away from him and Tahira and joined Maria, who was closest to the confabbing exec board.

"Okay. What do you think is going on with Lexa?" Ariana whispered.

"I don't know," Maria replied under her breath.

". . . acting crazy . . . ," Rob said.

"She's just under a lot of stress," Soomie defended.

"So are the rest of us," April put in, clearly hurt and pouting over it. "You don't see any of us freaking out."

"She really hasn't been sleeping at all," Maria added. "The other night I woke up at three a.m. and she was in the bathroom, scrubbing her hands. I mean, what's that about? It's like she's suddenly gone all OCD on us."

"Weird," Ariana agreed, swallowing back a new thump of dread. She was right about the imaginary blood. She knew it. She tilted her ear toward the group behind her.

". . . know I love the girl," Conrad was saying, "but this is unacceptable."

"He's right. We have to look out for Stone and Grave's larger interests," Palmer said.

"You guys, what're you saying?" Soomie asked fretfully. "You can't mean—"

"And then her mom called at six o'clock this morning," Maria said, drowning out Soomie's words. "I mean, the woman *knows* she's not sleeping, so she calls at the crack of dawn? What's that about?"

Ariana's fingers curled into fists over having a vital bit of the conversation spoken over, but she knew it didn't really matter. Because she knew in her heart of hearts what the execs were talking about. They were talking about removing Lexa as president of Stone and Grave. They were saying that if she didn't get her act together, she was going to lose her position of power.

Which meant that, as Lexa's best friend, she would lose any power she had in Stone and Grave as well—before she ever even got the chance to find out where that power could take her.

# BRINGER OF DRAMA

*What are you doing right now, Reed?* Ariana wondered, gritting her teeth as she stared down at the smudged photo in the newspaper, which was tucked inside her government text. *What are you doing right now? Are you having brunch with your friends? Is Noelle there? Are you still dating that Boy Scout Josh Hollis? What are you thinking? Do you ever even think about me? About what you did to me? About where I am right now, because of you?*

Someone dropped a heavy book on the other side of the stacks, and the slam brought Ariana back to the present. She heard someone curse under their breath as she looked around at the brightly lit Atherton-Pryce Hall library. The room was warm, thanks to a charming wood-burning fireplace in the corner, around which several students were gathered in plush chairs, their books splayed open across their laps. The sun streamed in through the skylights overhead, casting its beams along the spines of the classic, leather-bound books all around her. Ariana took a deep breath and sighed. Where she was right now actually wasn't that bad. Not bad at all.

It was what she was dealing with that scared her. She looked up, across the three tables that separated her from Lexa. This morning Lexa appeared to be just fine, all cuddled into her white turtleneck sweater, poring over her history text with Conrad. Every now and then, Conrad would run his hand over her hair and look at her with concern, whisper something in her ear, kiss her cheek. He was taking care of her, which was a plus. But Conrad had no idea exactly what he was dealing with—nor did Ariana want him to find out.

Lexa was dangling precariously over the edge of the deep end. The slightest mishap could push her in at any moment, and the splash would take out not only her, but Ariana as well. After what had happened the night before, Ariana knew what she had to do. She had to stick to Lexa like glue. She had to make sure that she stopped any future budding breakdowns before they could truly blossom. Otherwise, she was going to have to do something drastic. Something she didn't even want to think about.

"Hey. There you are."

Suddenly Palmer's arms enveloped her from behind. She slammed her government book closed over the newspaper, her pulse suddenly fluttering at an alarming rate. If Palmer had noticed that she was staring at an old sports section featuring girls' soccer, he was definitely going to ask her about it. What was she supposed to say? *I've suddenly developed an interest in women's sports?*

Palmer gave her a kiss on the cheek and lowered herself into the chair next to hers. His eyes flicked to Lexa and Conrad, and he gave Connie a nod.

"So. How's she been?" he asked Ariana.

Taking a deep breath, Ariana laid her government book aside, relieved, at least, that Reed wasn't about to become a topic of conversation.

"Okay. Fine," she said brightly. "They've been over there since before I arrived and not a peep."

"Good. That's good," Palmer said. Still, he kept his gaze on Lexa, as if he was mulling something over. Deciding whether or not to try to have her removed as president, perhaps? The very idea made Ariana sick to her stomach. Lexa loved being president of Stone and Grave. Having that taken away from her would only make her condition worse.

Not to mention that Ariana would never be able to exert her power over Lexa to get things done the way she wanted.

"You know, I was thinking about it last night and I realized . . . Lexa's actually been acting weird all semester," Palmer said, placing his elbows on the table. He turned toward Ariana and rested his cheek on his fist, as if trying to hide his words from the girl who was yards away.

"Really? How?" Ariana asked, preparing herself to refute anything he said.

"Well, first there was the cheating during welcome week," Palmer said. "That was not her style."

Ariana shifted uncomfortably in her seat. Lexa hadn't had anything to do with the cheating. Ariana had sabotaged one of the other boats for the crew race—and let Palmer blame it on Lexa.

"And then there was that whole thing with Lillian," Palmer continued.

Now Ariana's heart shifted into overdrive. "What whole thing with Lillian?"

"They way she just let Lillian in? Invited her to Stone and Grave?" Palmer said, lifting a shoulder. "We all told her she had to vet the girl, but she was all 'Lillian's good people. I like her. Case closed.' It wasn't until later when all the questions were raised about her that Lexa finally started to listen. And then, Lily up and disappears. I mean, how weird is that?"

Ariana forced herself to breathe slowly. Tried to figure out exactly how she was supposed to react to all of this—how a person who knew nothing about any of it would react.

"Well . . . Lillian leaving school . . . that had nothing to do with Lexa," Ariana said.

Palmer looked at her and narrowed his eyes. It was almost as if he was studying her. Almost as if he was thinking that Lillian's disappearance had something to do with . . . her.

"And then there's you," he said.

Ariana's heart stopped beating in her chest. Her mouth went dry, and she reached for her bottle of water, her mind racing. It was never good when people started to ask questions—when they started to really think about what was going on around them, trying to see the big picture. Clearly that was what Palmer was doing now. But how close was he to the truth? Did he really suspect Ariana, or was he just fishing?

"What do you mean, then there's me?" she asked slowly.

"Well, last year everything was normal. So I was trying to figure out what's different and then I realized . . . you are. You show up on campus and suddenly there's all this . . . drama," Palmer said, sitting back in his chair. "Are you a bringer of drama, Ana Covington?" he said, half-teasing, half-serious.

"Adam's new this year too," Ariana snapped. "Have you tracked him down and blamed him yet?"

Palmer blinked, surprised. "Sorry. I was just kidding," he said. "Thinking out loud."

Ariana clutched her water bottle. She stared at one little drop as it wound its way down from the mouth of the bottle and into the pool of untouched water at the bottom.

*Just focus,* she told herself. *Just breathe. Palmer doesn't know anything. How could he possibly know?*

She looked at Palmer out of the corner of her eye, hoping he would be the picture of chagrin. But instead, he was still watching her, as if he was trying to see inside of her. As if there was something odd there that he was trying to understand. This boy needed some serious distraction. And he needed it now.

"Look, I don't know if I'm a bringer of drama or what," Ariana said, turning her knees toward him. "But I do know that thinking out loud is a highly overrated pastime."

She lifted her leg, crooking it over his, and slid even closer. Palmer raised his eyebrows, intrigued.

"Oh yeah? Did you have some other activity in mind?" he said, slipping his arm around the back of her chair.

"Most definitely," she replied.

Then she leaned in and touched her lips to his, fully aware that the entire population of the library was watching them. She cupped her hand around the back of his neck and drew him into her, deepening the kiss and eliciting a moan from the back of his throat. Any second now, this was going to get broken up by one of the librarians, but until it did, Ariana was going to make sure that Palmer was good and distracted.

She was going to make him forget all about Ana Covington as a potential bringer of drama.

# NORMAL

"So that is when I told Fellini, if you want something done right . . . let me do it!" Maria's father said, his voice booming across the small parlor.

The small crowd that had gathered around Maria's parents laughed heartily, and Mr. Stanzini sipped his mimosa. His slim, couture-clad wife hung on to his arm, her huge sunglasses pushed casually back into her short brown hair. They were every bit as glamorous as Ariana had imagined, but she was having a hard time paying attention to this parental conversation too. She had lost sight of Lexa, which, considering they were standing in the very room where Kaitlynn's death had transpired, was very not good.

"Will you all excuse me for a moment, please?" Ariana said.

Mr. Stanzini nodded, which was enough for her. Ariana shook her head at a passing waiter as he offered another full tray of mimosas and ducked past Mr. Montgomery's elbow as he gestured his way through another story. She saw Jasper eye her with curiosity as she glanced around the room, but she ignored him. There were far more important things on her mind than Jasper and whatever it was he might be thinking.

Finally, out of the corner of her eye, Ariana saw a flash of red. She paused, and her heart squeezed. Lexa was walking through the yard outside the parlor windows. Walking toward the rose bushes.

*You let your guard down for two seconds . . .*

Ariana rushed to the French doors that led out to the garden. The sun shone down on the lazily falling leaves, and her feet crunched through them as she hurried to join her friend. The disarray of the yard was just another testament to the fact that they had chosen the right burial plot for Kaitlynn. Clearly no one ever came back here. It seemed that the Greenes had even neglected to hire a landscaper to rake the leaves.

Lexa stopped just inches from the recently turned-over earth. She reached up and toyed with her gold necklace, shivering as a cold November breeze rustled the bare branches of the rose bushes.

"What are you doing?" Ariana hissed, coming up behind her.

Lexa flinched but didn't turn to look at Ariana. Her gaze was trained on the base of the bushes. The exact spot where Kaitlynn's body now rotted away.

"Nothing," Lexa said. "Just . . . going for a walk."

Her bottom lip trembled, and tears brimmed in her eyes. Ariana felt the briefest pang of sympathy for Lexa—clearly the girl was not as strong as she'd originally hoped—but the sympathy quickly hardened into anger. This weakness could get them both in serious trouble.

"You need to relax," Ariana told her, standing just behind Lexa's shoulder. "Whoever Keiko hired to fix the window did a perfect job, and it's obvious no one's been back here and no one's coming back here. Unless, of course, they come out after us."

"I don't understand how you can be okay with all of this," Lexa whispered, not looking at Ariana. "It's like you're a robot or something."

Ariana's face warmed. "Thanks a lot."

"All I can think about when I stand here is the blood. All that blood," Lexa whispered, ignoring Ariana's comment. "It took forever for me to get it off my hands, and sometimes, it's like it's still there."

"Lexa," Ariana said in a warning tone. "I—"

"My life as I knew it . . . it's over," Lexa whispered harshly, turning to her. "It's ruined, all because of her. Because of—"

Behind them, someone opened a window, and laughter wafted its way toward them on the breeze.

"Lexa!" Ariana hissed through her teeth. "Your life is not ruined. Look around." She grabbed Lexa's arms and forcibly turned her, making her look back at the huge windows and the party going on behind them. "Your friends are still your friends. Your parents are doing just fine. Everything is just as it was, and do you know why? Because no one knows. And no one else will *ever* know. Unless *you* screw it up."

Lexa glanced at Ariana, her eyes wide, as if startled. As if it had never occurred to her until that moment that she was responsible for her own fate. Ariana could have smacked her across the face. Was she the only person around here who knew how to count on herself? Who knew that the future was all that mattered?

The French doors opened, and Lexa's mother peeked her head out. "Lexa! Briana Leigh! What are you doing out there without coats? It's freezing!"

"We'll be right there, Mother," Lexa said, sounding, thankfully, normal.

"Good. There are some people here your father would like you to meet," Mrs. Greene said. Then she closed the door with a bang.

Suddenly a tear spilled down Lexa's cheek. She clutched her arm and looked at Ariana, sucking in a broken breath.

"Everyone wants me to be normal," Lexa said. "But I don't know how I can be, Ana. I don't know . . . if I can live like this."

*I don't know if I can* let *you live like this,* Ariana thought, then flinched. The very idea of it pumped ice-cold fear through Ariana's veins. She didn't want to hurt Lexa. Lexa had been a good friend to her. And she didn't want any more blood on her hands. Not if she could help it. Especially not when she had finally gotten every last thing she wanted. She didn't want to have to do these things anymore. She wanted to live a normal life.

"Lexa, you'll be fine. I promise."

Lexa ducked her head, wiped her eyes with her fingertips, and speed-walked back toward the house. A stiff wind blew a pile of leaves up into the air, where they swirled for a moment before settling again around her feet—over Kaitlynn's grave.

Ariana turned her back to the house, clenched her jaw, and stared down at the ground, imagining Kaitlynn smiling up at her. Laughing at her.

"You're never going to stop causing me problems, are you?" Ariana said under her breath. She stomped once on the ground, seeing Kaitlynn's face beneath her stiletto boot. Then she turned on her heel and, feeling only marginally better, rejoined the party.

Unfortunately, she knew that she wasn't going to enjoy one second of it from that moment on. Because now she was going to spend the entire morning obsessing over plan B—a plan that she had yet to fully consider, hoping she wouldn't need it. Ariana sighed as she closed the door behind her and stepped into the warm parlor. *Stupid Ariana. You should know by now. You always,* always *need a plan B.*

# NEED

Ariana stood near the fireplace, sipping her mimosa as she watched Lexa socialize with their friends. The tears were gone, and she hadn't looked back toward the garden once.

Still, Ariana had made progress on her plan B. If she could find a way to make it all come together, she would have a safety net if the world of Briana Leigh Covington came crashing down. But that didn't mean she'd given up hope for plan A. Unfortunately, that plan involved Jasper, and he was nowhere to be found.

"Hey."

Suddenly someone grabbed Ariana's arm and whirled her around and through the open door to the dining room. The lights were dimmer in the wallpapered space, and as Jasper tugged her into the corner, Ariana felt suddenly closed off from the party.

*Speak of the devil,* Ariana thought.

She glanced past his shoulder toward the far end of the room, where Keiko and the chef were just disappearing through a pair of white doors leading to the kitchen. She and Jasper where completely alone.

"What are you doing?" Ariana demanded.

"I need to talk to you," Jasper replied. He stepped back, putting some distance between them, and Ariana felt slightly more comfortable. He was wearing a light blue shirt under a dark blue sport coat and jeans—the only jeans at the party—but at least he'd had the good sense to wear a pair of Brooks Brothers shoes and not sneakers.

"Good," she said, standing up straight and clearing her throat. "I need to talk to you, too."

Jasper hesitated, pressing a fist into his hand. His eyebrows arched, intrigued. "Okay. Ladies first."

"Okay," she said. She glanced back toward the door to the parlor, considering all the delicate ways she could put this. But then she remembered she was talking to Jasper. And Jasper always appreciated the straightforward approach. Besides, it would be better to get this over with. "Soomie wants to ask you to the ball. Any interest?"

Jasper blinked. His hands dropped to his sides. "That's what you wanted to talk to me about?"

"Yes," Ariana replied. She crossed her arms over her chest. "So do you like her or not?"

Slowly, Jasper's lips stretched into a sly smile. "Are you . . . jealous?"

Ariana's jaw dropped. "No, I'm not *jealous*," she replied. "I actually think it's kind of annoying how you're always flirting with me.

Especially considering that I have a boyfriend. And because, apparently, you like someone else."

Jasper took a step closer to her. The look on his face was one of pure self-satisfaction. "No," he said, "I do *not* like Soomie."

"Well, why not?" Ariana asked, frustrated now. "Soomie's incredible. She's smart and she's sophisticated and she's—"

"Not. You," Jasper said, carefully enunciating each word.

Everything stopped. Ariana looked into his eyes, and then her gaze flicked to his lips. She recovered quickly, but if Jasper's grin was any indication, he had seen her eyes shift.

"I notice le boyfriend is not in attendance," he said.

"He . . . he had to go do something with his parents," Ariana replied.

"Ah, what a good boy he is," Jasper said, moving even closer to her. So close their knees brushed. "I'm just curious as to why a girl like you would bother wasting her time with a guy like him."

Ariana's heart pounded in every inch of her body. Any second someone could walk in here and see them. See Jasper leaning toward her. See her looking up at him. Note the clandestine setting. Palmer would know in an instant. But still, she couldn't seem to pull herself away. "What do you mean, a guy like him?" she asked.

Jasper shook his head, as if the answer was so blatantly obvious. "Boring as white bread. Virtuous as a priest."

Ariana balked. "I'll have you know that he and I—"

Jasper held up a hand. "Spare me the unsavory details," he said. "I'm not talking about *that*. I'm talking about everything else. Do you think Palmer Liriano has ever done anything even remotely wrong? Remotely questionable. Remotely . . . naughty?" He looked her up and down in a way that made her blush all over. Then he grinned into her face. "Yeah. Didn't think so." He took a step closer, nudging her so far back her entire body was flat against the wall. "Let me tell you something, Ana Covington. Something I know about you that you may not know about yourself. You, my friend, need some excitement in your life. Some complexity. That guy? He's never going to be enough for you."

Ariana was so flustered she could hardly think straight, not a familiar sensation for her. She hated that she was letting him get to her.

"Not enough?" she asked finally. "Who could be better for me than the president of the student body? The second in command at S and G?" she said, lowering her voice. "Who could possibly have more to offer than the son of a professional athlete and one of the most respected congresswomen in the House?"

Jasper smiled slowly, looking directly into Ariana's eyes. His nose was mere millimeters from hers. The flap of his jacket lightly grazed the front of her brown dress. His eyes flicked to her lips, and Ariana felt her heart catch and her toes curl. "You need," he said quietly, "a guy like me."

Then he leaned in, closing the minute gap between their lips. For a wisp of a moment Ariana let go. She moved into him. But at the last second she lifted her hand, and all Jasper got to kiss were her fingers.

His eyes darted open, and he looked at her, stunned. Ariana felt proud, suddenly, for her self-control.

"Actually, there *is* something I need from you," she said. "I need you to get me a Valium prescription."

At that moment, a bell rang out in the parlor, the double doors behind Jasper opened, and out rushed the wait staff with bowls and plates full of steaming food.

"Brunch is served!" someone announced in the next room.

*Saved by the bell,* Ariana thought. And then, with a satisfied smirk and a quick smoothing of her skirt, she turned and walked away from him.

# BACKUP PLAN

At the third bail bonds storefront, in the bowels of Washington DC, Ariana finally struck pay dirt. There was a man there—if the troll she was faced with constituted a man—with the means of forging a very authentic-looking birth certificate. All he needed, he said, was ten thousand dollars. Cash. When he'd told her this, he'd done so with an evil, knowing, gap-toothed smile, as if he'd expected her to faint dead away. Instead, she had walked out, taken a bus to the nearest branch of her bank (she had decided not to bring her car into this particular part of town, since she would rather it not get stolen), and returned twenty minutes later with the money.

When the disgusting little man's watery eyes had widened, she'd felt a distinct hum of satisfaction in her bones. Now Ariana stood in the center of the grimiest room she'd ever had the distinct horror of entering, making sure not to touch a single surface as she waited for him to complete his work. She was certain that if she laid so much as a fingertip on the oil-smeared metal bookcases, the table littered with fast-food containers, or the walls with their pockmarks and unidentifiable stains, she would die of hepatitis on the spot.

"Here you go."

The man turned around from his cluttered desk, stubbing out a cigarette in an already overflowing ashtray. He exhaled two plumes of smoke as he handed over the green and white document that stated that Emma Jane Walsh had been born sixteen years prior on January 9 in Denver, Colorado. Ariana breathed a sigh of relief, ignoring the protestation in her lungs over having inhaled so many carcinogens while she waited. With this and the Emma Walsh driver's license she'd had made in Texas, she could get herself a real passport. And with a real passport, she would be able to flee the country if Lexa spilled about what had happed on Halloween.

"Thank you, Mr. Blaze," Ariana said curtly, folding the birth certificate into her bag.

"Pleasure doing business with you, sweetheart," he drawled, lighting another cigarette. He tore open the paper band around the stack of bills she'd brought him and started to count them. "Please come again."

*That'll be the day,* Ariana thought.

She used her elbow to shove open the swinging door of his office and speed-walked past the counter, where two middle-aged men turned away from the hockey game on TV long enough to leer at her. The second she stepped out into the frigid November air, she took a long, deep, cleansing breath. Everything was going to be fine. Her backup plan was in place. Then she looked up and down the seedy, semideserted street. A garbage can had been overturned near the wall, and a scraggly cat was picking through the debris, while two men all in black argued loudly near the corner.

Now all she had to do was live long enough for the bus to arrive. She sidestepped a swaying drunk and stood near the broken and graffitied bench at the bus stop. Her phone rang.

"Dammit," Ariana cursed under her breath, the life all but scared out of her. She dug her phone out and rolled her eyes when she saw Jasper's face on the screen. She hit the talk button and brought the phone to her ear.

"What?"

"Wow. Tense, are we?" Jasper replied.

"I'm kind of in the middle of something," Ariana said impatiently, eyeing a scary dude with a scar across his lip as he strolled by. He eyed her right back and puckered his lips at her. It was all Ariana could do to keep her lunch down. "What do you want?"

"Sushi," Jasper said. "Do you like sushi?"

Ariana forced herself not to turn around and follow the scary guy with her eyes as he passed behind her. She forced herself to train her eyes on the road. If he saw that his presence was making her tense, he might see that as an opening. A vulnerability.

"I went to your room to give you the Valium—it came, by the way—and to ask you if you felt like sushi, but you weren't there," Jasper was saying.

Scary Dude passed her by but turned around to walk backward, keeping his gaze on her as he made it to the end of the block.

"Fine. Pick me up in the next ten minutes," she said.

"Ana . . . where are you, exactly?" Jasper asked, suddenly sounding concerned.

Ariana's heart warmed, surprised and pleased that he'd picked up on her tone. She looked around for someplace, anyplace she could wait inside without fearing for her life at every second. She swallowed back bile when her eyes fell on the golden arches two streets down. "I'm at a McDonald's downtown," she told him. "I'll text you the cross streets."

Jasper laughed. "Never figured you for a junk food junkie."

"I'm not," Ariana snapped. "I just took a wrong turn." She looked over her shoulder at the bail bonds place, where Mr. Blaze and his two buddies were watching her, laughing.

*A very wrong turn,* she added to herself. She could only imagine what Noelle Lange and her other friends back at Easton would say if they knew the types of places she'd been forced to spend time in—the types of things she'd been forced to do.

"Just come get me," she said.

Then she snapped the phone closed and jogged across the street to the fast-food joint, resolving to never again get herself into a position that would land her back in this part of town.

# A GOOD LAUGH

"You need to try the spicy tuna," Jasper said, leaning across the table with a piece of sushi suspended between two chopsticks. He was wearing a black sweater that made his hair look even blonder and his blue eyes brighter.

"I'm not really a spicy person," she replied, pushing her rice around with her own chopsticks.

"Oh, I think you are. You just don't know it yet," Jasper told her. He popped the piece of sushi into his own mouth and raised his eyebrows as he chewed.

Ariana laughed, shaking her head. "Do you stay up nights coming up with these lines?"

Jasper grinned. "Not at all. You just bring them out of me."

"I'm not sure if that's a good thing or a bad thing," Ariana replied.

"Neither am I." Jasper took a sip of his sparkling water. "But I know you being here with me is a good thing."

Ariana looked down at her square white plate, her two sushi rolls arrayed beautifully across the surface. She and Jasper were, once again, seated on the floor, but this time she had the benefit of comfy suede pillows beneath her butt and soothing Japanese music playing through hidden speakers. Jasper had somehow scored them a private room at Kumo, one of the most exclusive sushi restaurants in DC, so they were completely closed off from the rest of the clientele by a set of sliding, opaque paper doors. The setting was secluded and completely relaxing—doubly so since the Valium prescription he'd brought her was nestled safely in her handbag. Plans A and B were progressing nicely.

"I don't know how I feel about being the inspiration for such behavior," Ariana said, hazarding a glance in his direction.

"Well, I would stop, if you would just let me kiss you already," Jasper said lightly.

"Why? Do you think that if you kissed me you'd stop feeling the need to pursue me?" she challenged, her heart fluttering.

"On the contrary," Jasper said, placing his chopsticks down. "If I kissed you, you'd be mine for life. And then I wouldn't have to pursue you anymore. I'd just have you."

Ariana's jaw dropped slightly. Every inch of her skin tingled as he stared directly into her eyes. She wasn't sure whether to be flattered or offended, intrigued or disgusted.

"You're staring at my lips again," Jasper said matter-of-factly.

Ariana started to protest, but stopped. "I know."

His eyebrows cocked. "Are your eyes trying to tell me something, Miss Covington?"

Ariana slowly smirked. "Just that you have a piece of rice stuck there," she said, blithely returning to her food.

Jasper flinched and wiped his face with his napkin, the moment effectively obliterated. Unable to hold it in, Ariana started to laugh. Then Jasper dropped his napkin and started to laugh as well. Soon they found they couldn't stop, and Ariana had to drop her chopsticks and cover her face, tears of mirth filling her eyes.

It had been a long while since she had laughed like that. So what if she was out on a date with a person who wasn't her boyfriend? It had been a long couple of years for Ariana Osgood.

And she deserved a good laugh.

# BOREDOM

"Did I really sound like that?" Lexa asked, pressing her hand against her chest. "I'm so sorry, you guys. But you heard my mother the other night. When I don't get enough sleep, I kind of lose it."

Lexa giggled as she tilted her head and rested it against Conrad's shoulder. Ariana smiled, happy to see that her friend was able to joke about her public breakdown. Maybe their little talk in the garden had worked.

"And besides, April should do her job," Lexa added, lifting a shoulder. "She's always showing off how organized she is. Well, guess what? She's not."

"Huh. Maybe you are a little OCD," Palmer joked.

Lexa shot him a look of death with her eyes, while smiling with her mouth.

"Just kidding," he said, raising his hands in surrender. "Honestly. I'm just glad you're feeling better, Lex."

"We all are," Conrad said, lifting his arm to place it around her on the back of her chair.

"How about we talk about something else?" Ariana suggested, dipping her fork into her mashed potatoes. "This restaurant is lovely. Have you ever been here before?"

The restaurant *was* nice, but bland. It had all the trappings of the basic, Washington, DC, steak house, the kind of place where politicos hung out after a long day of hashing out deals. The cream-colored walls were decorated with framed paintings of important moments in history; several deep, private booths flanked the dining room; and the lighting was low enough that a photographer might not be able to exactly make out who was sitting with whom. Ariana's steak had been fine, but a tad overcooked, so now she was concentrating on her sides. Her sides and her boyfriend. At least, she was trying.

"We come here every time my parents are in town," Palmer said, reaching for his wine glass. "Which is why they agreed to serve us this incredible bottle of Chardonnay."

"It *is* tasty," Lexa agreed, lifting her glass as well.

"I'm more of a red wine person, myself," Conrad said, taking a bite of his steak.

"Well, then, I'll have to become one too," Lexa said. She nudged his arm with hers flirtatiously and smiled up at him.

"They have some incredible reds here as well," Palmer offered, crossing his arms on the table. "The owner took my father and me on a tour of the wine cellar last summer. The whole thing really is fascinating. Wine collecting is definitely something I want to get into one day. Well, that and autographed baseballs. I already have a good collection of those going, thanks to my dad."

"Really? Who've you gotten?" Conrad asked.

Ariana cracked a smile as Palmer ran through the list, which was apparently impressive, if Conrad's oohs and aahs were any indication, but in the back of her mind she was envisioning a den full of sports paraphernalia—dirty jerseys encased in glass, banged-up baseballs set on custom shelves as if they had the same worth as diamonds. The whole idea made her skin crawl.

And why had she never noticed how much Palmer talked about his father? It was almost like he was name-dropping his own dad, showing off about the perks he could get because of who his father was. Jasper would never do anything so gauche.

*Stop it,* she told herself, placing her fork down and focusing her attention on the conversation. *Stop thinking about Jasper.*

"What about you, Lex?" Conrad asked, resting his wrists on the edge of the table as he looked at her. "What would you collect?"

"She just collects trophies and ribbons," Ariana put in proudly. "Have you seen her shelves full of equestrian awards, Connie? The girl's a natural."

"She's overexaggerating," Lexa said, blushing nonetheless.

"You know, I *have* seen those trophies, but I've yet to see you ride," Conrad said, turning his seat slightly toward Lexa. "When can we do that?"

"You should come to my family's ranch in the spring," Lexa said, her eyes sparkling. "I could show you a few moves."

Ariana was feeling more and more secure by the second. Flirting? Planning for the future? All of this was a very good sign.

Of course, she'd thought she'd seen a few good signs during their shopping excursion the week before, but Lexa had still backslid after that. The question was, how was she going to keep Lexa under control for good? Was she ever really going to feel truly safe as long as she shared this potentially life-ending secret with Lexa?

"You know, Ana, you should come visit me at home this summer, too," Palmer said, reaching for her hand under the table. He clasped it and brought it up to rest on his thigh. "I'd love to show you around Phoenix."

Phoenix. Blah. Could there be any place on earth more unappealing in the dead of summer than the middle of the desert? Ariana wondered where Jasper spent his summers. Hadn't he said something about his father owning real estate all over the world? And now she did too. Maybe the two of them could go vacation-home-hopping around the globe together.

"Ana?" Palmer prodded.

Ariana blinked, dragging herself back from a gondola in Venice, wrapped in Jasper's arms.

"What? Oh, sorry. Sure. Of course. I'd love to see Phoenix," she lied.

"Will you guys excuse me for a second?" Lexa asked, rising.

Both Conrad and Palmer got up from their chairs, well-trained gentlemen that they were. Lexa sauntered off toward the bathroom. The second she was out of earshot, Conrad leaned across the table.

"She keeps bringing up Lillian," he whispered to Palmer. "Do you think that has something to do with all the crazy hand washing?"

Ariana's blood froze in her veins. "What has she been saying about Lillian?" she asked, even though she was appalled by the fact that Lexa's boyfriend started talking about her behind her back the second she was gone.

"Nothing in particular," Conrad said, lifting a shoulder. "But she keeps reminiscing about the girl. As if they were lifelong friends or something. We only knew her for a month."

"Maybe she's wigged about Lillian leaving so abruptly," Palmer said, looking off in the direction of the bathrooms. He narrowed his eyes. "Maybe . . . maybe she found out something about Lily's mystery family that she hasn't told us! Maybe she doesn't think that Lillian left because she couldn't handle the workload."

"What do you mean?" Ariana asked, breathless. She could barely believe she was having this conversation.

"Maybe she suspects foul play," Palmer said.

Ariana laughed, but the sound was shrill. "Foul play? What is this, *Harriet the Spy*?"

Palmer turned up his palms. "We all thought it was sketchy that we couldn't find anything out about Lillian's family. Maybe they were connected. Like to the mob or something."

"Whatever you say," Ariana said, rolling her eyes in an exaggerated way. She hoped they couldn't see her heart pounding through her flimsy dress material.

"Whatever," Palmer said, frustrated. "All I know is, if that's the case, I'm glad the girl's gone. The last thing we need is to be friends with someone who's caught up in a scandal."

Ariana felt an uncomfortable twist in her gut. "Why? What's the big deal?"

Palmer took a sip of his wine and placed the glass down next to his bread plate. "It's just that I don't think I could ever be friends with someone who'd let themselves get involved with stuff like that."

Ariana felt as if she'd been slapped. "Sometimes it's not the person's fault, you know. Sometimes the situation is out of their control. Stuff happens."

Palmer and Conrad both snorted laughs. "That's the lamest excuse in the book."

Lexa returned to the table at that moment, all smiles, and the guys greeted her happily, as if nothing had been discussed in her absence other than Ariana and Palmer's lame upcoming trip to Phoenix. Ariana took a long swig of her wine and sat back, annoyed. She couldn't believe Palmer could be so judgmental, could dismiss her argument out of hand like that. She knew better than anyone that sometimes bad things happened to good people. If he didn't understand that, then what kind of person was she dating?

As Palmer launched into the list of things they could do together in Phoenix—catch a Diamondbacks game, go for a hike in the desert, see a concert at Red Rocks, where his dad had a permanent box—Ariana couldn't help wondering what Jasper was doing right then.

And how much more fun he was having doing it.

# FINE

"So . . . what are you working on, exactly?" Ariana asked Soomie as she and Lexa stepped into their friend's room after returning from their double date.

Soomie blew out a frustrated sigh and dropped a hole punch on the floor with a clatter. She sat in the center of her wool throw rug, surrounded by strips of pale wood, bottles of glue, scissors, an X-Acto knife, and a set of blueprints. Her normally sleek hair was back in a messy bun, but half of it had fallen out in stringy clumps around her face.

"She's supposed to make a balsa-wood plane for physics class," Maria replied. She was leaning back against the desk chair, her arms crossed over her chest. "I think Mr. Crandal has finally found the project to stump the great Soomie Ahn."

"He has not," Soomie snapped. "I don't care if I have to stay up all night. This thing will win."

Maria raised her hands in surrender as Ariana and Lexa exchanged disturbed and amused glances. Soomie reached for a section of balsa wood that appeared to be fashioned into a plane's wing. Her finger shook, and Ariana saw that her palm was sweaty. This project was obviously stressing out Soomie.

"Do you need any help?" Lexa asked.

Soomie shot her a look that could have killed Frankenstein's monster in his tracks.

"Don't ask her that," Maria said, shaking her head. "I nearly lost a finger asking her that."

Soomie returned to her work, and Maria sighed. "Let's talk about something else. How was your date?"

"It was incredible," Lexa said, giddily looking to Ariana for confirmation. All Ariana could muster was a tight smile. "I thought it was going to be tense, but I had a great time."

"Yeah," Ariana said. "Me too."

"Ow! Sonofa—Shit!" Soomie cursed through clenched teeth.

Ariana looked up. There was blood everywhere. Soomie held her wrist tightly, a serious slice right across her palm. She'd dropped the X-Acto knife on the floor, and her meticulous blueprints were now spotted with blood.

"Omigod! Soomie! What did you do?" Maria demanded.

She looked around wildly and grabbed a clean T-shirt out of Soomie's laundry basket, where perfect stacks of folded clothes waited to be put away in the closet. Maria felt to her knees and wrapped the T-shirt around Soomie's hand. It was soaked through almost instantly.

"We have to get her to the infirmary," Ariana said as Maria helped a shaky Soomie to her feet.

"No!" Lexa blurted. She dropped the heavy frame on the floor, where it cracked into three pieces.

"What?" Maria and Ariana said in unison.

For the first time, Ariana got a look at Lexa. She clutched her hair at her temples with both hands, knotting up her brown tresses into two little rats' nests. Her eyes were like tiny pinpricks as she stared at the bloodstained floor. Her skin was as pale and translucent as white gauze.

"Lex, it's okay," Soomie said weakly. "It's just a little blood."

"Come on, Lexa. Why don't you sit down," Ariana said, hoping against hope the girl would listen to her.

"No!" Lexa screamed "No no no no no!"

She turned around and ran. Ariana took one look at Maria—who supported Soomie around the waist, and Soomie, who was bent over and looking faint—then took off after Lexa.

*This is not happening,* Ariana told herself, rushing for the doorway as the tail of Lexa's red coat disappeared around it. *This is* not *happening. It's all a bad dream, and any second I'll wake up safe and happy in my bed.*

"I have to get out of here!" Lexa shouted, tearing down the north hallway and pounding on the doors and walls as she went, like a wild woman. "I have to get out of here! I have to get out of here!"

"Lexa, stop!" Ariana shouted. She grabbed Lexa's arm, and Lexa whirled around, slapping Ariana dead across the face. Her eye exploded in pain, as if it was being ripped from its socket. Ariana's knees hit the floor as she held her shaking hand to her face. But still Lexa kept running

"What the hell is going on?" Tahira demanded, opening the door of her room. The moment she saw Ariana on the ground she stooped to help her up. "Ana! Are you okay?" Tahira's roommate, Allison Rothaus, stepped tentatively into the doorway in pajama pants and a tank.

"Lexa has completely lost it," Maria said, helping Soomie into the hall.

"Oh my God! What happened to *you*?" Allison asked Soomie.

"I have to get out of here!" Lexa screamed before anyone could answer. "I have to get out of here!"

Ariana couldn't have agreed more. She had to get Lexa out of there before she said something, anything that might incriminate either of them.

Down in the lounge, Lexa started to pound on the plate-glass windows with both fists. A large pane rattled angrily as the reflections in its surface bent and contorted.

"Shit," Tahira blurted. "If she breaks one of those windows . . ."

Ariana, Tahira, and Allison raced to the lounge, where Tahira made a move for Lexa's arms.

"I wouldn't do that if you want to keep all your teeth," Ariana said, which made Allison freeze in her tracks.

"Don't worry," Tahira told her, holding out one hand flat. "I got this."

She took Lexa's right arm from behind, then ducked when Lexa whirled around. With the deftness of a karate black belt, Tahira grabbed Lexa's left arm as well and held her two arms clasped together at the wrist.

"It's okay, Lexa. It's just me," Tahira said in a loud but soothing voice.

"Let go of me!" Lexa raved, squirming like mad. "Let go! I have to get out of here!"

"Lexa, you don't need to go anywhere," Tahira said, keeping a firm grip on her with both hands and looking her directly in the eye. "You need to come sit down."

Ariana hovered in the entryway, watching in awe as Tahira attempted to calm their friend. She had no idea Tahira was so strong.

"Why are you doing this to me?" Lexa whined, still trying to wrest herself out of Tahira's grasp. "Why are you trying to hurt me?"

*God, just shut up!* Ariana screamed silently, her cheekbone still throbbing with pain while her eye stung. *Shut up before you say something I can't explain away.* She clasped her forearm in her hand, squeezing with all her might in order to keep herself in check—to keep herself from lashing out in the name of self-preservation. There was nothing she could do right now. Not with all these people watching. But if she and Lexa had been alone right then . . . Ariana wasn't entirely sure she would be able to control herself.

"No one's trying to hurt you, Lex," Ariana said, stepping forward. She slowly, carefully, put her arms around Lexa. "We're your friends. We're trying to help you."

"My friends try to hurt me," Lexa said, her voice turning meek. She looked down at the floor, letting Ariana and Tahira lead her over to one of the cushy leather couches. Together the three of them sat, but it wasn't until Lexa rested her head on Ariana's shoulder that Tahira finally released her.

"No one's trying to hurt you, Lexa. I promise," Ariana said, stroking Lexa's hair. Lexa closed her eyes, and Ariana looked up at Soomie and Maria, who hovered in the door.

"You guys should go to the infirmary," Ariana said. "I can take care of her."

"You sure?" Maria asked.

"Yeah. Just go. Soomie's not looking too well," Ariana said. "No offense."

Soomie shook her head slowly and swallowed. "None taken."

The two girls shuffled off toward the elevator and Allison, probably feeling like an outsider among friends, silently returned to her room.

"What happened?" Tahira asked, standing up.

"I don't know. Soomie cut herself, and Lexa completely freaked out," Ariana said honestly.

"I guess some people can't handle the sight of blood," Tahira said.

"No, I guess not," Ariana replied.

But most people fainted. Or threw up. Or walked out of the room. Lexa was acting as if she needed to be committed. She was acting even crazier than most of the women inside the Brenda T. Trumball Correctional Facility on their worst days. Why did this have to happen?

Why now? She had thought Lexa was fine. But now it was clear that anything could set the girl off at any time. Suddenly Ariana felt completely and utterly defeated.

"Should we try to take her back to her room? Put her to bed?" Tahira suggested.

"Actually, maybe she should stay in my room for the night," Ariana said, standing up straight. "Who knows when Maria will get back. I think someone needs to keep an eye on her."

"You do have the extra bed," Tahira pointed out, tilting her head. "Maybe a solid night's sleep will be good for her. Why don't you see if you can get her over there and I'll go get her some pj's."

"Okay," Ariana said. "Come on, Lex. You're gonna stay in my room tonight, okay?" She stood up slowly, dragging a blinking Lexa with her.

"Okay," Lexa replied, her voice a touch pouty.

Ariana slipped her arm around Lexa's and shuffled her toward her room. Tahira went down the hall to Lexa's room and let herself in. As soon as the she was gone, Ariana quickened her steps, got to her room, and closed the door behind her and Lexa.

"Lex, I'm going to give you something to help you sleep," she said. She walked to her desk and extracted the small, orange bottle from the very back. Shaking out a couple of Valiums, she fumbled inside her mini-fridge for a bottle of water. "Here."

"What is it?" Lexa asked, narrowing her eyes as she gazed at the small pills in Ariana's palm.

"Just a little Valium so you can rest," Ariana told her, dumping the pills into Lexa's hand. "You need your sleep, right? Your mother said so, *you* said so. This is going to make you feel so much better."

"Okay," Lexa said. "I *could* really use some sleep."

Then she popped the pills into her mouth and reached for the bottle of water. After a few quick slugs, she slumped a bit, her eyes closing halfway.

"See? You're so tired," Ariana said. "Why don't you lie down?"

Lexa nodded twice, slowly. She started to sit down on Kaitlynn's bed, but halfway there, her eyes flew open, and she popped up again, as if zapped by an electric shock.

"That's her bed. I can't sleep in her bed. I can't. I can't, Ana. I can't!"

Ariana gritted her teeth and said a quick prayer for patience. "Okay! It's okay!" she said to Lexa, gently taking her arm. "You don't have to. You can sleep in my bed."

The moment the words were out of her mouth, Lexa calmed down again. Ariana led her across the small room to the bed on the opposite side. Lexa lay down, resting her head on Ariana's custom pillow. In about two seconds her eyes were closed, and ten seconds after that, she was snoring. Ariana knew that the Valium hadn't had time to kick in, but she was sure that Lexa was exhausted. Maybe she'd just needed a little prodding to get to sleep. And once the Valium *did* kick in, it would *keep* her asleep. Maybe it would even make her feel more rested—more like herself—in the morning.

At least Ariana hoped it would. Because she wasn't sure how much more of this particular Lexa she could take.

# SEIZING THE MOMENT

*What am I going to do? What am I going to do?*

Ariana glanced over at her bed, where Lexa snored deeply. Then her eyes trailed to her desk drawer. Inside were her many bankbooks. The keys to several safety deposit boxes that held untold millions' worth of jewels. And the copy of her birth certificate. Her Emma Walsh birth certificate, the original of which was already in the mail to the passport agency with her rush order for a new passport. Ariana didn't want to run. She'd created a life for herself here. A life she treasured.

But she would run. If she had to.

Taking a deep breath, Ariana turned and looked up at the ceiling again. She tried to imagine up a new life for herself. A life as Emma Walsh. Where would she go? If Lexa broke her silence and compromised her Briana Leigh identity, Ariana wouldn't be able to flee to any of Briana Leigh's homes. But if she was able to get back to Texas and grab the jewels, she could sell them for enough cash to open a significant account under her new name and then . . . then she could choose her country, choose her new home.

Ariana's heart thumped. She clasped her chenille blanket—the one that was usually tossed at the bottom of her bed for decoration and did not lend much warmth—closer to her chest. Suddenly she felt overwhelmed by a yawning sense of loneliness. The great, wide world spread out before her, full of strangers, void of friends. After all she'd been through, would she really have to start all over again? Would she really have to say good-bye to everything—and everyone—she'd come to love?

There was a creak, and Ariana's head popped up off the pillow. Her door slowly opened, and a booted foot stepped into the room. Ariana's chest constricted, and she sat up straight, lunging for the lamp on Kaitlynn's desk. Her fingers had just closed around the cold brass stand when Jasper's blond hair came into view.

He looked at Ariana's bed in confusion, then his eyes darted across the room and fell on her. Suddenly Ariana realized she must look pretty ridiculous sitting in an almost bare bed, her toes exposed, as she clutched a blanket and a lamp like a crazy paranoid person.

"What are you doing?" they both whispered in unison.

Ariana rolled her eyes, replaced the lamp, and flung her blanket aside. Lexa gave a loud snort and rolled over onto her side. For a split second, both Ariana and Jasper froze. Then the cadence of Lexa's breath returned to normal. Ariana tiptoed across the room, grabbed Jasper by the wrist, and pulled him out into the hall. His skin was cold, and his breath was shallow and ragged, as if he'd just run up the stairs and was trying to hide the effects.

"Why is Lexa sleeping in your bed?" Jasper asked.

"Why are you sneaking into my room?" Ariana demanded.

Her own heartbeat was still normalizing after the fright he'd given her. She looked up and down the hall, which, since it was three in the morning, was blissfully quiet.

Jasper smirked and leaned back against the wall. He wore dark blue jeans and a gray crewneck sweater, and his cheeks were ruddy, as if he'd just come in from outside. No wonder his skin was frigid to the touch. What was he doing outside in the middle of the night? He looked her flannel pajamas up and down, and her face burned as he took in the colorful polka dots.

"Nice jammies."

Ariana crossed her arms over her chest self-consciously. "Jasper—"

"I wanted to see how your date went," he said matter-of-factly.

Ariana's eyes darted to the floor, as the irritation, humiliation, and boredom of the night washed over her anew. She still couldn't believe how narrow-minded Palmer was.

"It went fine, thanks," she replied.

"That good, huh?" he joked.

Ariana had had just about enough of this. All this flirting. This coyness. This childishness. It might have been cute a week ago, but now things had changed. Now, with the potential end of this world looming, she didn't have time for such things. She looked up again, looked Jasper in the eye, and felt suddenly desperate. Desperate for some honest, straightforward truth.

"Jasper," she said firmly, "what are you really doing here?"

The smile fell from his face. His eyes grew serious.

"Seizing the moment," Jasper said. He reached up and touched her lips with his thumb, cupping his other fingers around her chin. Ariana froze, feeling his touch in every inch of her body. Her heart pounded in her ears.

"Jasper," she whispered harshly.

"Just shut up," he said.

And then he kissed her.

# NO CONTROL

"Lexa, where are you going?"

Everyone at the lunch table looked at Ariana, who realized with an embarrassed pang that she had maybe blurted that question a tad too loudly. Lexa paused, half out of her chair at the head of the table.

"To the bathroom," she said flatly.

Ariana shoved her chair back. "I'll come with you."

She dropped her sandwich, placed her napkin alongside her plate, and got up. She hadn't let Lexa out of her sight for a second all day. She just couldn't risk it. Not until she made sure the girl was stable. Or decided what, exactly, to do if she wasn't.

As Ariana followed Lexa to the end of the table and out into the aisle, all she could think about was the fact that the crazy behavior had to stop. She didn't want to forge a new life for herself. She wanted to live *this* one.

Even if it didn't come to that—even if Lexa never mentioned a word about Kaitlynn, even if her ramblings continued to be non-specific, they had to stop. Because one more nonspecific public ram-bling was going to get her ousted as president of Stone and Grave. And Ariana couldn't have that. She wasn't sure what she wanted to use Lexa's power for yet, but she knew it was going to come in handy one day. It would be nice if she had some time to figure out how.

"So, you had Ferren for English last year, right?" Ariana asked as the two girls made their way around chair legs and tossed backpacks.

"God. Don't remind me," Lexa replied, rolling her eyes.

"I know! She really likes to have a lot of grades in before the end of the term."

"Seriously," Lexa said, hugging herself. "It's like the first half of the semester there's barely any work, and then she suddenly starts piling it on."

"At least she assigns good books," Ariana said. Small talk was so very normal. So very not crazy. "There's not one I haven't enjoyed reading."

Lexa shoved open the swinging door that led to the lobby and the bathrooms beyond. She held it so that Ariana could walk through first "Right. But it doesn't matter if you like them or not. What matters is whether or not you can remember every character and their motiva-tion."

"Is that what the test will be about?" Ariana asked, following Lexa over to the bathroom.

"Yep. Trust me. Make a character list, and write down exactly why each one of them did what they did. It's the best way to study." She started into the bathroom, but paused. "Oh, and make sure you get the spellings right. She'll dock you points for misspellings."

"Noted," Ariana said.

At that moment, the side door to the building swung open, and Jasper walked in. Ariana's heart skipped an excited, anticipatory beat, but it was quickly extinguished by guilt. The kissing the night before . . . it had been amazing. But it had also been wrong. Very wrong. She was with Palmer. And Ariana was a lot of things, but she'd never been a cheater.

Ariana glanced at Lexa, who waited just inside the bathroom. Part of her hesitated, not wanting to leave Lexa alone for even a second. But the bathroom appeared empty, and Jasper was sauntering toward her.

Lexa couldn't spontaneously confess to anyone in the bathroom if there was no one to spontaneously confess to, right?

"I'll be in in a sec," she told Lexa.

"Okay." Lexa let the door close, and Ariana turned to face Jasper.

"Hey," he said, pausing in front of her with a smile. This time it wasn't sly, but comfortable. As if he was settling in because he now knew where he stood. Which just made her feel even guiltier, this time over what she was about to do to *him*.

"Hey," she said tentatively.

"So listen, I've been thinking about your double date last night," Jasper said.

Ariana blinked. That was unexpected.

"And you know what I think?" He tilted his head, one hand in the pocket of his slacks.

"Um, what?" Ariana asked, taken off guard.

He took a step, closing the gap between them, reached out, and fingered the lapel on her APH blazer, rubbing the fabric between his fingertips. Ariana suddenly found herself breathless. "I think that tonight *you* should meet up with *me*. Because *I* . . . will show you a good time. Unlike some people."

Ariana glanced toward the heavy wooden doors that separated her and Jasper from the dozens of people in the dining hall. If that door opened, someone would see. Someone would catch her and Jasper standing so close together their breath was mingling. And just like that, her relationship with Palmer would be over.

For one terrifying moment, a piece of her actually wished it would just happen. Wished the doors would open and the end result would be out of her hands.

And the fact that she wished it would happen—the fact that she wished, in that moment, for a lack of control—was what scared her. Jasper brought that out in her. Just as Thomas had. She couldn't do that to herself again. And she couldn't do it to Palmer either.

"I can't," she said, taking a step backward. "I have a study date with Palmer."

Jasper's face fell ever so briefly, and then he smiled. "Okay," he said. "If that's how you really want to spend your time. But just so you know, I don't have a date with anyone. And if you want me, I'll be waiting."

# BABYSITTER

Ariana knew that she had to keep an eye on Lexa, but she drew the line at inviting her along on her study date with Palmer. A foursome had been fine, but a threesome would be nothing but awkward. Which meant there was only one thing for her to do.

She needed to find a babysitter.

Which was why she left her government class five minutes early, had Quinn meet her with a latte and a coffee with sugar, and positioned herself outside Conrad's calculus classroom two seconds before the bell rang. Lexa seemed to be herself around Conrad, for the most part, as long as they were one on one and not surrounded by a crowd. Ariana wasn't sure if Conrad's presence calmed the girl or if she was working hard to impress him, but it didn't matter. She knew she would feel safe if Lexa spent the night alone with her boyfriend.

"Hey, Connie!"

Ariana stepped forward the moment his broad shoulders filled the doorway. He paused and gave her a confused smile. "Hey, Ana. What're you doing here?"

"I left class early for a caffeine fix because I was falling asleep, but the guy at the Hill gave me the wrong cup and I had to reorder," Ariana lied smoothly. "He was going to dump it out, but then I remembered you like black coffee with light sugar, right?"

She held the cup out to him with a beatific smile.

"Wow," he said, accepting it. "Good memory. Thanks."

Ariana lifted a shoulder and kept her eyes on him as she sipped her latte. "I pay attention to details."

The rest of the class was parting around the two of them as they stood right in front of the door. Ariana caught a couple of curious glances from April and Christian, but they kept walking.

"So, got any plans for tonight?" Ariana asked. She turned and started slowly down the hallway, and Connie fell into step with her.

"Not really," Connie said with a shrug. "Probably just studying. Why?"

"Oh, nothing, it's just . . . I think Lexa could use some quality boyfriend time," Ariana said. "If you're not doing anything, maybe you guys could go out."

Conrad paused at the top of the stairs, stepping aside to let a couple of teachers pass them by.

"Did she say something to you?" Conrad asked, taking a sip of his coffee.

"No, just . . . like I said, I pay attention to details," Ariana replied.

"She's been down lately, and I just know that being with you makes her happy."

Conrad's face broke out in a grin that could have stopped traffic. "It does?"

"Of course. She really likes you, Conrad," Ariana assured him. "And I think you've been really good through everything that's been going on with her. Clearly you're a stand-up guy."

Taking a sip of his coffee, Conrad seemed to mull all of this over. "Well, I wouldn't want to lose my reputation as a stand-up guy," he said finally. He gave her a light tap on the arm, which almost knocked her over. "Thanks, Ana. I'll take her out tonight."

"Cool. Have fun!" Ariana called after him as he descended the stairs.

He lifted his coffee by way of a good-bye, then disappeared out the front door. Ariana smiled to herself over a job well done. Babysitter acquired. And all for the small price of a cup of coffee.

# LESS CONFUSING

"Okay, here's an easy one," Palmer whispered, leaning toward Ariana across the corner of the table they shared in the library that night. "Which amendment started prohibition and which amendment ended it?"

Ariana stared across the packed library study section at the glowing green exit sign above the door. When Jasper had said he'd be waiting, did he mean in general, like waiting for her to break up with Palmer, or did he really mean he'd be waiting for her tonight? Was he back at Privilege House right now, actually, physically waiting for her?

"Ana?"

Ariana blinked and looked at Palmer. God, he was gorgeous. His brow knit in concern, and he reached for her hand under the table. His palm was warm as he cupped her fingers atop her leg. His fingers brushed her skin just under the hem of her skirt. Two weeks ago that contact would have sent her skyrocketing through the ceiling. Now all she could think about was Jasper's hands. Jasper's fingers. Jasper's touch on her thighs. . . . What was wrong with her?

"Are you okay?" Palmer asked. "You seem kind of out of it."

"Do I?" Ariana asked, tucking her hair behind her ear. "I'm sorry. It's just . . . I can't stop thinking about the English exam I have on Friday. Lexa told me what to do to study for it, and I just think I should be doing that right now."

Palmer leaned back in his chair. "Oh, okay. Yeah, I guess this can wait."

Ariana started to gather her things. Suddenly she felt almost panicked to get back to Privilege House. To just be by herself, in her room, where things were infinitely less confusing.

"It's just, I feel like I have the government stuff down, but for the English . . . there are just so many books. I really think I need to start making notes," Ariana told him. She slammed her heavy government book closed, and the noise drew attention from all the neighboring tables.

"No problem. Do what you've gotta do," Palmer said. He stood up as she stood up and planted a quick kiss on her lips. "I'll call you later."

"Okay. Cool. Bye," Ariana said.

And she was out the door without a second glance. She struggled outside with her unorganized books and notebooks, her laptop weighing down her bag against her hip. Then she hoofed it up the hill to Privilege House.

Once in the elevators, Ariana tapped her foot impatiently. The ride seemed to take forever. When the doors finally slid open, Ariana ducked out and sprinted for her room. Inside, she dropped her bags on the floor and turned to switch on the light, but before she could, a hand came down over her mouth.

# THE ONE

Ariana's heart leaped into her throat. She opened her mouth to bite down on the hand, but then she inhaled and stopped. It was Jasper. She could smell his piney cologne.

"Shhhhh," he said in her ear, his chin brushing her neck from behind.

Ariana pressed her lips together to keep from giggling with relief. Then a blindfold fell over her eyes and was tied tightly at the back of her skull. She felt a brief twinge of fear mixed with annoyance over being manipulated, but then decided she didn't care.

And just like that she surrendered herself to him. She relished the feeling of his strong grasp on her arms as he turned her around and led her silently through the door. She basked in the fact that she trusted him completely—that she was letting him do what he would. It was in that moment that Ariana knew, truly knew, that she was falling in deep.

Because there was no one, absolutely no one, for whom Ariana Osgood was willing to lose control.

At least, no one who was still breathing.

Finally the blindfold slipped from Ariana's eyes, tickling her cheek as it fell. She gasped when she saw the spread before her. The large movie screen standing near the edge of the roof. The piles of pillows and blankets strewn across the floor. The stars twinkling overhead. She turned to Jasper, and he smiled. He was wearing a gray sweater and a black coat, and looked so handsome Ariana wanted to melt.

"Jasper. This is amazing," she said.

"I know," he replied with a self-satisfied grin.

Ariana clucked her tongue and rolled her eyes. "How did you do this without anyone seeing?" she asked. Then her heart skipped a frightened beat. "No one saw you, right?"

"Of course not," he said. "Stealth is my middle name."

"But what if someone comes up here?" she asked, her eyes darting to the door. "What if—"

Jasper closed the distance between them and pressed one finger to her lips. "No one ever comes up here between the months of October and April. May, June, and September are another story, since apparently the girls around here are still interested in contracting skin cancer. But November? Don't worry about it."

Ariana took a deep breath and let herself relax slightly. She turned and walked around a low brick wall that ran across the center of the roof. She noticed that some of the pillows had been propped up against it on the other side, forming a makeshift couch.

"You do realize that we have a movie theater right downstairs," Ariana teased, lifting one of the velvety red pillows. "As I recall it's supposed to be one of the privileges of living in Privilege House."

"Privilege my ass. Do you know what they're showing down there right now?" Jasper said, walking around to join her. "*Avatar.*"

Ariana snorted a laugh.

He walked over to the projector and hit a button, bringing the machine to life. "I, however, have a *real* movie on tap."

Suddenly the screen flickered to life, and Ariana saw the familiar opening scene of *Breakfast at Tiffany's*. Audrey Hepburn traipsed along the New York streets in her black dress and tiara, smiling her bright Hepburn smile. Ariana sighed contentedly. Audrey Hepburn was her favorite actress of all time, and this was the greatest of all her films.

"Shall we?" he said, gesturing at the ground.

"We shall," Ariana replied giddily.

They sat next to each other, and Jasper reached around for the bottle of champagne he'd stashed nearby. He popped the top, and Ariana squealed as foam sprayed out, soaking one of the blankets near their feet.

"Sorry about that," Jasper said, looking not at all sorry.

"I'll bet," Ariana replied, gently wiping her toes with her fingertips.

"I've been thinking," Jasper said, holding the bottle between them. "You should come to my soccer game on Friday."

Ariana pulled a baffled face. "And why would I want to do that?"

Jasper lifted a shoulder. "Because I am excellent at soccer. If you saw me play you wouldn't be able to resist me."

"You'd be surprised at my capacity for self-control," Ariana replied smoothly, even though just being this close to him was making her nerves sizzle and her mouth water.

Jasper didn't respond. He simply smirked, as if he knew she was exaggerating. "Also, I think you should come home with me for Thanksgiving next week."

Ariana blinked, unable to contain her surprise. Thanksgiving was big. Thanksgiving was the kind of holiday one only attended if things were serious. "Really?"

"Yeah. I mean . . . with your grandmother gone and everything . . . it might be a little depressing to go home," Jasper said. "And we have a huge party. My family comes from all over, and we cook all weekend and eat and drink and dance. You'd love it."

"Nothing depressing about that," Ariana replied with a smile.

She hadn't even thought about where she might go when the school closed down for Thanksgiving break. But now she realized it might be nice to go down south. Almost like going to her real home. And she'd never gotten the chance to meet Jasper's parents over the weekend.

"Okay," she said, feeling all warm and fuzzy inside. "I'll think about it." She glanced down at the open champagne bottle. "Are we going to be drinking that anytime soon?"

Jasper smiled. He brought the bottle to his lips, taking a long drink. Then he offered it to her.

"What? No glasses?" Ariana asked.

"Afraid you're going to catch my cooties?" Jasper asked, raising one eyebrow.

"Oh, I think we're well beyond that," Ariana said.

Normally not one for drinking and the surrender of control that inevitably occurred, Ariana decided this was a special occasion. She took the bottle from him and allowed herself one good sip. When she lowered it again, she looked at Jasper, holding his gaze, then licked the tingling liquid from her lips.

Jasper smiled slowly. "You know exactly what you're doing, don't you, Ana Covington?"

"Always," Ariana replied.

And then she leaned forward and kissed him. And as Jasper turned toward her, as he slipped one hand around her neck and the other inside her coat and over her flat stomach, something flipped inside Ariana, and she just let herself go. She stopped thinking. Stopped planning. Stopped wondering what it would all mean. Stopped wondering how she would break up with Palmer. For once she just let herself feel.

She felt his lips pressing firmly against hers. Felt the cold touch of his hand as it slid beneath her shirt and lay against her warm skin. Felt her body arching toward his, wanting to know every single inch of him. When his lips left hers and trailed over her cheek, down her neck and onto her shoulder, she felt as if she might explode with happiness.

Jasper knew what he was doing. It was as if he knew exactly where she wanted to be kissed. Exactly *how* she wanted to be kissed.

"I've wanted to do this since I first saw you," Jasper whispered in her ear, sending delicious shivers down her spine.

"When did you first see me?" Ariana breathed, her eyes closed, her leg wrapping around his waist.

"The first day here. Out on the quad when we got our colors. You were with your friends, and you looked so damned gorgeous," he said, gasping for air as he kissed her. "Every second since then I've been dreaming about this."

Ariana brought her mouth down on his and kissed him like she'd never kissed anyone before.

Suddenly Jasper pulled back. One hand cupped her face and the other was on her thigh. His lips were pink and raw, and his breath was quick, but he seemed suddenly, perfectly serious. He looked into Ariana's eyes, his own so clear they were almost startling.

"I love you," he said firmly.

Ariana blinked. There was no hemming and hawing. No "I think I'm falling for you." No "I can totally imagine myself loving you." None of those vague, hedgy things boys usually said to give themselves a safety net. This was not a statement he was going to back away from anytime soon. But that was Jasper. He knew who he was. He knew who he wanted. And the person he wanted was Ariana.

*No. The person he wants is Briana Leigh Covington.*

And suddenly tears sprung to Ariana's eyes. She pressed her hands into the blanket at her sides and scooted herself away from him.

"What's wrong?" he asked.

"You can't say that," she told him. "You don't even know me. Not really."

Without hesitation, Jasper closed the gap between them. He took both her hands in his and sat cross-legged, looking at her openly. "I can say that. Because even though I might not know every little thing about you, I know there's nothing you could ever do, nothing you could ever say, that would make me *not* love you."

Ariana's jaw dropped slightly. He couldn't have said anything more perfect if he'd had a thousand screenwriters working for him. How did he know? How was he always able to do and say exactly what she needed him to do and say at any given moment? Suddenly Ariana was back at that restaurant table with Palmer. Hearing him say that he could never be friends with anyone who'd let themselves get involved in a scandal. If Palmer knew who she really was, he'd drop her in a second. But Jasper . . . Jasper was going to love her no matter what. A tear spilled out over her cheek, and Jasper reached up, touching it away with the pad of his thumb.

Ariana opened her mouth to speak. "I—"

The sound of squealing car tires split the air, followed by a shout of surprise and a scream. Ariana and Jasper looked at one another, startled, then jumped up and ran to the side of the roof. A black Cadillac Escalade whipped around the turn in the parking lot below and into a spot where it slammed on its brakes, sending smoke and the scent of burning rubber into the air.

"Isn't that Royce's car?" Jasper said.

*Oh crap.*

Conrad hurled himself out of the front seat, slamming the door so hard it was a miracle the thing didn't fall off its hinges.

"I have to go," Ariana said without a second thought.

"Wait. Why?" Jasper asked.

But Ariana was already gone, sprinting down the stairs toward the first floor of Privilege House as fast as her quaking legs could carry her.

# BAD THINGS

"Connie!" Ariana said, gasping for breath as he slammed the front door of the dorm. She'd just made it to the lobby as he stormed inside—and right past her on his way to the elevators. "Conrad!"

Connie completely ignored her and stepped into the waiting elevator. She heard him curse under his breath as he drove his fists into the back wall with a bang. Ariana's heart was in her throat. What had happened? Where was Lexa? What had she done?

Dear God, what had she *said*?

Blindly, Ariana shoved open the door and ran for the parking lot— ran for Conrad's car. From three feet away she saw Lexa doubled over in the front seat, bawling her eyes out, her long dark hair half covering her blotchy, tear-stained face. Ariana sprinted over and tried the door. It wouldn't budge.

"Lexa!" Ariana shouted.

The girl continued to cry, rocking forward and back, forward and back. Ariana's pulse raced so fast she thought she was going to black out. Instead, she gripped the door handle with everything she had in her and forced herself to focus.

"Lexa!" she shouted, slamming both palms flat against the thick window glass. "Lexa! Open the door! Lexa, honey you've gotta unlock the door!" She began to beat the pane with the heels of her hands, making so much noise she couldn't possibly be ignored.

Lexa looked up then, her hair sticking to the snot under her nose. Her eyelashes were thick with tears, and her eyes were shot through with red lines.

"I can't get it out, Ana," she said, her words muffled by the thick glass. "I can't get it out."

Slowly, Ariana's gaze fell to Lexa's hands. She was wringing them together as if she was trying to wash them.

"I can't get it out, Ana. I can't get it out."

Ariana flashed back to tenth-grade English and *Macbeth*. Lexa was channeling Lady Macbeth in her breakdown scene. Ariana remembered Leanne Shore reading the soliloquy in class like it was yesterday. "'Out, damn'd spot. Out, I say!'"

*She's crazy. She's really and truly crazy,* Ariana thought, her heart sinking like a stone. She had a sudden vivid memory of Crazy Cathy back at the Brenda T. One afternoon the inmates had been enjoying their outdoor time when suddenly Cathy had started screaming. She'd jumped up from her table and fallen to the grass, writhing and shouting that there were ants on her skin. That she was covered in them. That they were crawling up her nose and into her ears and over her brain. She'd had to be locked down in solitary for over a week, where she'd screamed herself so hoarse her voice had never been the same.

Lexa had that same look in her eye that Cathy had that day. Like she wasn't really there. Not there at all. Ariana had counted on the fact that Conrad's presence would keep her calm, but if she could have a breakdown like this even when she was alone with him, then Ariana was in serious trouble. Because she couldn't keep watch over Lexa 24-7 for the rest of her life. It simply could not be done.

*Don't think about that. Not yet. Right now all you have to do is bring her back. And you* can *bring her back,* Ariana told herself. *You* have *to bring her back.*

"Lexa, please," Ariana said calmly. "Just hit the button with the little open lock on it, right there. Right there on the door. Hit it so I can open the door and get you out of there."

Lexa sniffled and looked down. "I can't get it out."

Ariana swallowed hard. Lexa didn't even understand her.

And then, suddenly, a click. Ariana's head popped up. She reached for the door handle and tried it again. The door swung open. Lexa looked at her, her back bent, her shoulders curled.

"I can't get it out," she said.

"I know," Ariana said soothingly, reaching for her. "I know, Lex. I'm gonna help you."

Carefully, she tugged Lexa out of the huge SUV. The moment Lexa's high heels met the ground, her ankles went out, and she almost hit the asphalt. Cursing under her breath, Ariana braced her arm under Lexa's and held her up. She was heavier than she looked. Ariana looked up at the glowing windows of Privilege House, wondering where the hell Conrad had gone—why he hadn't come back out to check on Lexa. Did he even realize she was still out here?

"Come on. Let's get you inside," Ariana said patiently.

"I can't get it out, Ana," Lexa said, holding her shaking hands out flat as she loped along. Her fingers were all dry and cracked from so much washing, and her palms were red and raw. But there was nothing staining her hands. Nothing to be gotten out. "I can't. I just can't get it out. No matter what I do, I can't get it out."

"I understand," Ariana assured her, holding Lexa close to her side. "I understand."

Lexa caught a few curious and appalled looks from a group of sophomore girls as Ariana helped her to the elevator. It was all Ariana could do to keep from lashing out at them. This could just as easily have been them. No one around here knew how close they all teetered to the abyss. They all thought they were so secure, so wealthy, so privileged that nothing could ever touch them.

But they didn't know. They had no idea. No one was safe. Bad things could happen to anyone at any time.

"I can't get it out, Ana. I just can't get it out," Lexa whimpered as the elevator whisked them to the top floor.

"I know, Lexa," Ariana replied, stroking her hair. "I understand."

Tiptoeing as best she could so as not to arouse the attention of their other friends, who would undoubtedly pepper her with questions, Ariana escorted Lexa to her room. She helped her lie down on her bed and removed her shoes, placing them carefully on the floor.

Then she fished out her almost full bottle of Valium and stood next
to the bed.

"I can't get it out, Ana. I can't get it out."

Ariana stared at the dozens of tiny pills inside the bottle. It would
be so easy. Lexa was completely out of it. All she had to do was feed
her the pills. Surely an entire bottle of Valium could take care of one
tiny person like Lexa. She would simply swallow them, go to sleep,
and never wake up. It would be like putting a dog out of its misery.
Look at the girl. She was a disgusting, sad, sorry mess. She wasn't
in her right mind. Probably never would be again. And when they
found her in the morning, Ariana could just say that Lexa must have
taken the pills herself while Ariana slept. It would be so . . . very . . .
easy.

Slowly, Ariana uncapped the bottle. She tilted it over her palm and
shook out two of the small, white pills.

"Here. Take these," she told Lexa, holding out her palm.

Lexa looked at the pills, focusing for the first time all night.
"They'll help me sleep," she said robotically.

"Yes. They'll help you sleep," Ariana replied.

Obediently, Lexa swallowed the pills dry, then curled up on her
side on Ariana's bed, facing the wall. Ariana placed the cap back on
the bottle and shoved it as far back in her drawer as it would go. Then
she closed the drawer slowly and moved her chair over to block it from
opening. To remind her that it was not to be touched.

"I can't get it out, Ana. No matter what I do. I can't get it out."

Ariana lifted the chenille blanket from the foot of her bed. She laid it over Lexa, then crawled into bed behind her, looping her arm around Lexa's waist.

"I can't get it out Ana. I can't get it out."

"I know, Lexa. I understand. Don't worry. Everything's going to be okay. I'm going to take care of you."

And Ariana held Lexa close, until the Valium finally did its job and she drifted off to sleep.

# AWARE

The next morning, Conrad was sitting at one of the indoor tables at the Privilege House café, sipping a coffee and staring down at a novel that he had open across one thigh. Ariana watched him for a couple of minutes. Every once in a while he shook his head, as if irritated, and refocused on the book, gritting his teeth. Ariana knew exactly what he was doing—reading the same line over and over again because he couldn't concentrate. Because he was thinking about Lexa.

*You shouldn't have bailed on her,* she thought, clenching her jaw. *If you were going to feel so guilty about it, you shouldn't have deserted her, locked in your car.*

Stealing herself, Ariana walked through the lobby and over to his table. She had to keep reminding herself that Conrad was not a villain in all of this. He didn't know how to handle the new Lexa any better than anyone else. All he needed was a little help. A little guidance.

Maybe, in fact, a bit of guilt. And Ariana was going to be the one to help him feel it.

"Hey," she said, pausing behind the wire-backed chair across from his. "How's it going?"

Conrad's eyes flicked over her face. "It's going." He returned his attention to the page.

"Mind if I sit?" Ariana asked. She didn't wait for a reply. "So much for being a stand-up guy," she said.

Conrad sighed and closed his book, dog-earring his page as he laid it flat on the table.

"I guess you talked to Lexa," he said derisively. "Oh wait, you couldn't have, because she's frickin' out of her skull."

"Conrad," Ariana said, gripping the marble tabletop with both hands as she glanced around at the other occupied tables. "Please."

"Why keep my voice down? Everyone knows it, Ana," Conrad said, lowering his voice nonetheless as he leaned forward. "The girl is in need of some serious drugs."

*Which she's already getting,* Ariana thought.

"No, she's not. She's just going through a tough time," Ariana said.

Conrad sighed. He leaned back heavily in his chair and shook his head, as if Ariana was saying exactly what he didn't want to hear. Ariana's blood started to boil with impatience. Maybe he *was* the villain.

"What, exactly, happened last night?" she asked.

"We went out to this restaurant that I knew would serve us wine. You know, because of all that stuff the other night about her becoming a red wine girl and all that?" he said. Ariana nodded and he leaned forward again, resting his forearms against the edge of the table like a well-mannered gentleman. "So I picked out a great bottle, and we ordered our food, and everything was fine. But ten minutes into the meal I knocked over her wine glass by mistake, and she went completely off the reservation."

Ariana swallowed hard. Spilled wine. Like spilled blood. That's what had done it. It wasn't much of a leap to make when one knew the whole story.

"She starts wringing her hands together and talking about how it's never gonna come out," Conrad said, speaking more rapidly as the story tumbled forth. "So I'm telling her it's just a tablecloth and who cares and they'll get us a new one, but that just seems to rile her up until she's screaming. 'I can't get it out! I can't get it out!' It was a total scene. We got thrown out of the damn place."

"God, Conrad. I'm so sorry. That must have been awful," Ariana said, trying to keep the sarcasm out of her voice. He had no idea how much worse it could have been. No idea the level of crap *she* had endured for the past two years—the sort of awful, humiliating episodes she'd had to live through thanks to Reed and Thomas and Kaitlynn.

Her fingers clenched under the table as the photo of Reed from the paper, happy, athletic Reed—the only one of the three who was still alive—flashed through her mind. She shoved it away. It was not about Reed right now.

"Yeah! It was!" he replied indignantly.

"Now how about you think for two seconds about how Lexa felt?" Ariana shot back.

Conrad stared at her. He picked at his linen napkin on the table absently. "What do you mean?"

"Obviously she's going through something, Conrad. Otherwise she never would have acted that way," Ariana said, leaning back and crossing her slim arms over her chest. "You know Lexa. She's the most polite, well-spoken, self-aware person we know. Obviously something has to be seriously wrong for her to do something like that. But instead of trying to understand, instead of trying to talk to her and take care of her like a boyfriend should, you left her locked in your car in the parking lot."

Ariana's hands curled together in her lap again. Her fingernails cut into her fleshy palms.

"Wait, she was locked in?" Conrad said, a smidgen of concern crossing his face for the first time. "I didn't know. I must've hit the button by mistake."

"Either way. Do you really think that was the right thing to do? To just leave her there like that?" Ariana asked him.

Conrad blinked. He looked down at his cooling coffee. "No. I guess not. But still. You didn't see her. I—"

"I *did* see her," Ariana interrupted. "I'm the one who got her out of the car. I'm the one who helped her inside and up to bed and made sure she was all right—all things you should have been doing if you had a single chivalrous bone in your body."

"Wow. Tell me how you really feel," Conrad said, trying for a light tone, but looking stricken.

"I think I have," Ariana replied, rising from her chair. "I suggest you stick by your girlfriend. Give her a second chance. Otherwise I'm not sure your conscience will ever forgive you."

Then she turned her back on Conrad's dumbfounded face. Shaking her head as she walked away, it was all she could do not to hurl a string of curses back at him. She'd always thought that Conrad was such a good guy, but apparently she was wrong. Still, he'd have to do for now. He was all Lexa had. Once she got back on an even keel she could break up with him and find a real man. A good man. Someone who would stand by her, no matter what. In the meantime, Ariana would take that role. She'd be there for Lexa. Someone had to be.

Ariana whipped out her cell phone in the lobby. She hit a speed dial button, lifted the phone to her ear, and shoved open the door, stepping into the frigid November morning.

"Beaura Day Spa," a woman answered in a clipped tone.

"Yes. I'd like to make a reservation for this Saturday for a full spa day for five people."

There was a condescending laugh on the other end of the line. "Miss, I'm not sure if you're aware, but we're always booked months in advance, and Saturday is obviously our busiest day."

"Oh, I'm aware," Ariana replied, tossing her hair off her cheek. "Now let me make *you* aware of exactly how much money I'm prepared to spend."

# ILLUMINATING

Ariana leaned back in the heavenly leather pedicure chair at the day spa, a cooling cucumber mask slathered over her face, while her hands were massaged by her manicurist, a diminutive woman named Shelly, while her feet soaked in bubbly rose water, prepping her for her pedicure. Surrounding her in four identical chairs, enjoying four identical treatments, were Lexa, Maria, Soomie, and Tahira. They were all wrapped snugly into deep red terry-cloth robes, and Ariana felt gooey and relaxed after the most intense full-body massage she'd ever experienced. It turned out that once the Beaura Day Spa heard exactly what Ariana had in mind for today, they'd had a miraculous number of appointments open up.

It was good to be Briana Leigh Covington.

"So, Soomie, whatever happened with Jasper?" Lexa asked, resting her head back against her neck cushion.

Instantly, Ariana tensed up. Her manicurist paused, noticing it.

Ariana cleared her throat and forced herself to relax, embarrassed over the idea that this stranger might be able to read her body language. She shot Shelly a relaxed smile and told herself that the important development here was that Lexa was engaging with her friends. That she was interested, alert, and aware.

Very not crazylike.

"I don't know," Soomie said. She turned her hand over casually, checking her white gauze bandage. "Ana, whatever happened with Jasper?"

Ariana's throat closed over. What did Soomie know? What had she seen? But then, as the other girls looked at her expectantly, she realized that Soomie meant something else entirely. Ariana was supposed to talk to Jasper for her. Which she'd done. Almost a week ago.

"I'm so sorry, Soomie," she said. "I . . . I've been so busy. I just never got the chance to talk to him."

"If he's not interested you can just tell me," Soomie said moodily. "I'm a big girl."

Ariana bit her lip, snagged. Her cheeks were aflame. "It's not that—"

"Whatever. I should have just gotten up the guts to ask him myself," Soomie said, leaning her head back against the small leather pillow.

Suddenly Ariana felt the touch of Jasper's lips on hers. Tasted his tongue. Felt his hands on her stomach. It was like every cell in her body was pulling her toward Jasper. Pulling her toward his confidence, his sexiness, his mystery, his sense of adventure, his willingness to break the rules. He may not have been the wise choice, but her heart, her soul, her body . . . all of her wanted him. She tensed up again, and her manicurist raised one eyebrow. Ariana blushed and looked away.

"Well, there's still time," Maria said, lifting her fingernails to check her black nail polish. "The ball's tomorrow night. I say call him right now and ask him."

Ariana bit down on her bottom lip to keep from protesting. Because how was she supposed to support her protest without sounding jealous? She racked her brain for a reason that Jasper might be unsuitable for Soomie but could think of nothing. Probably because Jasper was so very, very perfect.

"Easy for you to say," Soomie said. She glanced at Tahira in the next chair. "People in long-term relationships always forget how hard it is to put yourself out there."

"So true," Tahira replied, then blew on her fingernails.

Ariana's heart stopped. She glanced at Maria, whose eyes were wide and startled.

"What do you mean? What long-term relationship?" she asked. "I haven't even hooked up with anyone since the summer."

"God, Maria, everyone knows you and Landon are together," Tahira said, rolling her eyes. "Who do you think you're kidding?"

"What?" Maria blurted, sitting up. She almost knocked over a tray full of lemon water one of the waitresses was toting around from chair to chair. "We're not—"

Lexa laughed, shaking her head. "Maria, just stop," she said. "We're your best friends. Of course we know."

"Really? Are we still best friends?" Soomie interjected.

Ariana's body heat skyrocketed as Lexa balked. "What do you mean?" Lexa asked.

"It's just that you haven't been around much lately, Lex," Maria said, shifting in her seat. "And clearly you've been upset about something, but clearly it's not something you're willing to share with us," she added, giving Ariana a pointed look.

Lexa cleared her throat, looking down at her hand for a moment, as her manicurist shaped her nails. "I'm sorry, you guys. I know I've been a little . . . out of it lately. It's not really something I'm . . . ready to talk about," she said, glancing quickly at Ariana. "But I'm feeling better. I swear. And if it was something I thought you should know, I promise I would tell you."

There was a long moment of silence. Ariana breathed in and out, relishing Lexa's perfectly reasonable and coherent answer. Maybe she really was getting better.

"As long as you know we're here for you, Lex. No matter what," Soomie said.

"I know," Lexa replied quietly. "Thanks, guys."

This time, the silence was far less tense, far more companionable. Then, out of nowhere, Maria blurted, "So you guys all *know*?"

Everyone laughed. "Maria! Why do you think I gave him Pip?" Lexa said. "He was supposed to be Dr. Jekyll, originally. You know, because he has the whole split-personality thing going. Of course, with Landon it's the private and public personas rather than the sane and the batcrap crazy, but it still would've worked."

Everyone froze. Lexa had just mentioned a Stone and Grave secret in public. There were a dozen spa workers in the room, every one of them within hearing distance. Ariana glanced around surreptitiously, but none of the manicurists, facialists, or waitresses seemed remotely interested in what was being said. She let out a sigh of relief, then almost laughed. Of course, they wouldn't be interested. How would any of them have any idea what it meant to give someone Pip? They probably thought it was some new drug they'd never heard of.

"I can't believe this," Maria said, dropping back again and closing her eyes in resignation. "How long have you known?"

"He and some of the other guys were down at the boathouse before Soomie's Halloween party and he blabbed then," Lexa replied, waving a dismissive hand. "We've known for days."

"I wish you'd told me you knew," Maria complained with a pout. "Do you know how hard it is to keep a secret around here?"

"Apparently too hard," Ariana joked.

Everyone laughed, and Ariana was just relaxing, happy that the subject had turned away from Soomie and Jasper, and that Lexa had just offhandedly mentioned Halloween night without freaking out and running screaming from the room, when her cell phone beeped. She fished it out of the pocket of her robe with her free hand—the one that wasn't currently being polished. There was a text message from Jasper himself. Ariana's pulse began to pound, and her palms started to sweat. She glanced quickly at Soomie, as if the girl could read her phone from across the room. Soomie was still teasing Maria, so Ariana opened the text.

WHERE R U? THOUGHT U WERE COMIN 2 MY GAME

Ariana's heart stopped, and she dropped the phone. It slid off her knee and dropped toward the footbath. Ariana lunged for it, but Shelly's hand shot out and caught it at the last second.

"Thank you," Ariana breathed.

"Uh huh," the manicurist said knowingly, handing the device back to her.

Ariana blushed. "Can I have my hand for a second?"

"Of course," Shelly said, releasing her.

Ariana pursed her lips and texted back.

I AM SOOOOO SORRY! CONNIE BROKE UP W/ LEXA + SHE NEEDED ME. U UNDERSTAND RIGHT?

She hit send and sat back to wait. The manicurist looked up at Ariana from her little stool, watching her with discerning eyes. Ariana ignored her and tried to tune in to her friends' conversations while she waited. And waited. And waited. The more time went by, the more Ariana's underarms began to prickle with nervous sweat.

Was Jasper ignoring her text? Was he that mad at her for forgetting?

Then, mercifully, her phone beeped.

OK. 2 BAD THO. U SHOULDA BEEN HERE. WAS V ILLUMINATING.

Ariana's brow knit. Illuminating? How could a soccer game be illuminating? She was about to text him back and ask him that question, when her phone beeped yet again. Another text from Jasper.

SO WHEN R U BREAKING UP W/ CAPTAIN BORING?

Ariana rolled her eyes, smiled, and hit ignore.

Shelly had a tight-lipped smile on as Ariana offered her hand again. "Texting the boyfriend?" she said slyly.

"Oh, that's so nauseating!" Tahira teased. "Palmer can't even be away from you for a few hours."

Ariana blushed and lowered her lashes. "What can I say? He needs me," she lied.

Shelly shook her head and sighed as she started applying a topcoat to Ariana's nails.

"Ah, young love. I remember what that was like. I think."

Ariana, Soomie, and Lexa laughed, while Tahira and Maria made skeptical faces.

"How do you know it's love?" Tahira asked Shelly. "Maybe she's just in lust."

"Oh, no. It's love. I can tell by the look on her face," Shelly joked back.

Ariana grinned. She really was falling for Jasper. Even the help could tell. The question now was, what was she going to do about it?

She lifted her phone and quickly texted back.

JUST GIVE ME SOME TIME TO FIGURE IT ALL OUT.

The answer came almost instantly.

HOW MUCH TIME?

Ariana smirked, flattered by his impatience. She texted back.

I'LL GIVE YOU AN ANSWER AT THE BALL.

# DEFINITE IMPROVEMENT

"Ana, you look drop-dead in that gown," Tahira said as the girls walked down the hall to the elevator on Saturday evening. "I hope you know a good dry cleaner because Palmer is going to drool all over it."

"Thanks, T," she said, grinning.

*But I'm no longer in the market for Palmer's drool,* she thought, imagining how Jasper was going to react when he saw her stepping out of the elevator. She had decided that tonight was the night. She was going to break up with Palmer at the ball, where he wouldn't make a scene, where he would have plenty of alcohol in which to drown his sorrows, and plenty of friends around to drown them with.

And where she could disappear in the crowd with Jasper afterward. Because she knew that as soon as the deed was done, she wouldn't be able to wait another second to be with him.

Ariana stood in front of the floor-to-ceiling windows in the lounge area, checking her hazy reflection in the glass, turning this way and that to see the full skirt of her gunmetal gray, strapless taffeta gown swish around her. The skirt was wide and stiff and accentuated her tiny waist. She'd adorned her neck with a real diamond necklace she'd purchased at Cartier the day before. Noelle had one just like it—except hers was peppered with sapphires—which she always used to wear to the Ryans' Casino Night party down on St. Barth's over Christmas break. Ariana smirked slightly, wishing her old friend could see her, could know who her friends were, how much she was worth. It was next to impossible to make Noelle Lange jealous, but Ariana had a feeling that she'd actually turn green if she knew. And green was so not her color.

"You're looking pretty drool-worthy yourself," Ariana added.

Tahira had gone with a low-cut, black velvet dress that hugged every curve. Ariana wasn't a big fan of the leave-nothing-to-the-imagination look, but it was very Tahira, and Ariana was slowly starting to get used to her new friend's style.

Tahira executed a twirl, holding her silver clutch purse out at her sides. "I know," she replied, lifting one bare shoulder.

"Everyone ready?" Lexa asked, sweeping out in her black gown.

Ariana smiled with satisfaction at the sight of her friend, who looked well-rested and happy. Her skin glowed, and she was eye-circle-free for the first time in days. Maybe the massage and facial had really relaxed her enough for her to get a good night's sleep. Maria trailed behind her in a silver halter-neck dress, her arm crowded with at least ten diamond tennis bracelets. Then Soomie emerged in a tight, black-and-gray-striped strapless with an ankle-length pencil skirt and a slit

up the back. Her dark hair was pulled back into a coil at the nape of
her neck.

"Damn, we clean up well," Maria said, looping her arm around
Soomie's.

"We do, don't we?" Lexa added, taking Maria's other arm.

"Well, we're already fifteen minutes late," Ariana said, checking
her phone. "The boys should be sufficiently agitated."

The girls giggled as Ariana led them to the elevator. Her heart beat
a nervous rhythm as she hoped that Jasper would be waiting down-
stairs with the others. She knew Palmer would be there, as planned.
As would Landon, Rob, Conrad, and Adam, who had agreed to be
Soomie's date. But maybe Jasper would want to see her first thing too.
She hoped so.

"The guys just have no idea what it's like for us," Maria said as the
elevator whisked them toward the lobby. "All the things we put our-
selves through to look this hot. All they have to do is shave, put on a
tux, and done."

"And some don't even bother to shave," Tahira groused, giving the
bodice of her dress a tug.

The girls giggled as the doors slid open. Ariana stepped out and
immediately scanned the couple dozen tuxedoed boys for a shock
of blond hair, but Jasper was nowhere to be found. Her heart was
just sinking with disappointment as Palmer stepped forward, his eyes
gleaming with unabashed admiration.

"You look gorgeous," he told her, giving her a quick kiss. He
hugged her, and as Ariana rested her chin on his shoulder, she gave the

room another cursory glance. No Jasper. Where was he? Why wasn't he here? Was this some kind of payback for not showing up at his game the day before? He was still coming to the ball, wasn't he?

"Thanks," Ariana replied as Palmer released her. She tried to smile. "You do too."

"Thanks," Palmer said, tilting his head. "Everything okay?"

Ariana flicked her bangs away from her forehead. "Yeah. Fine. I'm just—"

The words died in her throat. Out of the corner of her eye she glimpsed a flash of red. Her heart withered inside her chest as she saw Conrad Royce striding across the lobby toward Lexa, a huge bouquet of red roses clasped in one hand. There had to be three dozen of them—big, fat blooms, so crimson they could have been dyed with blood. He was taking Ariana's advice. Trying to make it up to his girlfriend. But he couldn't have picked a more inopportune method for an apology.

Roses. Bloodred roses. Just like the ones currently forming a canopy over Kaitlynn Nottingham's grave.

A few feet away, Lexa's back was to Conrad. Maria and Landon noticed him approaching, and Maria's entire face lit up. She touched Lexa's arm to turn her around, and Ariana briefly closed her eyes. She couldn't take this. She simply could not watch.

"Hey, Lex. These are for you."

"Oh my God," Lexa said.

Ariana watched the back of her eyelids and awaited the breakdown.

"Ana? Are you okay?" Palmer said, gripping her elbow.

"Oh my God, Conrad!" Lexa squealed. "They're beautiful! Thank you!"

Ariana's eyes fluttered open. It took her a moment to focus, but when she did, Lexa and Conrad were hugging, and Maria was leaning back to keep from getting hit in the nose with the flowers.

"I know I said this before, but I'm really sorry about the other night," Conrad said. "Do over?"

Lexa beamed up at him. She took the roses in both hands and lowered her face to the blooms, taking a deep breath to inhale their scent.

"You've got it," she told him.

Ariana let out a breath, and suddenly her heart was so giddy she could hardly contain it. Clearly Lexa had turned a corner. Clearly she was getting better. Because if the sight of roses didn't make her think of Kaitlynn, if they didn't make her freak out the same way red wine and the blood and the broken glass had, that was definitely an improvement. Everything was going to be all right. Everything was going to be fine. In a few short hours, she'd have everything she'd ever wanted.

"Oh, man. Are you mad that I didn't get you flowers, too?" Palmer said, reaching for her hand. "I didn't think this was a flowers occasion."

"No, it's okay," Ariana said, squeezing his hand and thinking of Jasper. "It's all good."

"Good," Palmer replied. "Next time I promise to outdo Conrad."

He released her, looped his arms around her waist, and leaned in for a kiss. As she kissed him back she decided it wasn't a betrayal because, as Soomie would put it, (A) he was still her boyfriend, (B) she'd just gotten very good news, and (C) Jasper wasn't here to see it anyway.

Plus, there was always (D) every relationship deserved a good-bye kiss. And Palmer didn't know it yet, but that's exactly what this was.

# VERY BAD GIRLS

"What an incredible venue for a party," Ariana mused, looking up at the stars trough the glass roof of the massive greenhouse at Maria's parents' Alexandria mansion.

"Apparently the previous owner had a serious green thumb," Trent Greenway informed her, spinning the brandy in his glass. Mr. Greenway was a world-famous movie producer who'd had at least one multimillion-dollar hit a year for the past ten years, or so Lexa had informed Ariana right before she'd introduced them. Ariana had never been a huge modern film buff, but the list of hits had impressed even her. "Rudolpho and Cordelia have no such interest, so they cleared it out, put in the marble floor, and have used it for parties ever since."

"It's got nothing on the ballroom at your place, though, Mr. Greenway," Lexa said, tossing her hair over her shoulder. "You have to see it one day, Ana. Mr. Greenway has this amazing, sprawling place in the hills overlooking Hollywood, and the ballroom is right on the cliff."

"Wow. Sounds amazing," Ariana said.

"It is. The wife begged me not to build it. Something about an earthquake hazard," he said. "But she wasn't complaining after our last Oscar party got her picture in all the rags."

"Besides, one more hit like *Flicker* and you can build yourself another," Lexa said with a laugh.

Ariana blinked, appalled for a moment. She thought it was gauche to mention success and money to an adult. But Trent Greenway simply laughed. Apparently he liked to have his success and wealth bandied about publicly. And apparently Lexa knew this. Suddenly Ariana was reminded of how good it was to know someone like Lexa—someone who knew all the right people and knew how to handle them and herself.

"I've said it before and I'll say it again, Miss Greene. If you're ever interested in a career in the movie business, give me a call," Mr. Greenway said with a genuine smile. "I could use someone like you around the office." Then he looked at Ariana. "You too, Miss Covington. You've got that creative yet ruthless air about you. Both qualities would work well for you in Hollywood."

Ariana was stunned into speechlessness.

"Ladies," he said with a bow, removing himself from their space. He backed away and struck up a conversation with Landon and Maria. Lexa smiled at Ariana, impressed.

"I know!" Ariana said, moving toward the bar. The skirt of her dress scraped delicately along the floor, and the cool air circulating around her tickled her skin. "But where'd he get ruthless from?"

"I told him how you stole Palmer from me," Lexa said matter-of-factly, resting her empty glass on the bar and signaling for another. "Maybe he was referring to that."

Ariana's jaw dropped. "Lexa, I—"

"I'm just kidding!" Lexa said, placing her hand on Ariana's arm in a placating way. "You should see your face. That joke is just never going to get old."

Ariana rolled her eyes and leaned back against the bar, biting back a retort about how the joke had gotten old the first time it was made. But what was the point in arguing about this now? She had a feeling the jibe would be completely passé the moment she broke up with Palmer, and then she'd never have to hear it, or explain it, or feel guilty about it again.

Not that she had ever felt all that guilty about stealing Palmer from Lexa in the first place. She'd simply done what needed to be done.

As Lexa sipped her new drink, Ariana was suddenly hit with a brilliant idea. Perhaps Lexa and Palmer would get back together. The moment she imagined it, she was shot through with automatic jealousy, but in the next moment she realized how silly that was. She didn't want Palmer anymore. And he was a good guy. He and Lexa had been in love once. They could be again. Ariana realized it might be difficult for Palmer to get over her, but once he did, he could be exactly what Lexa needed. Solid, mature, kind, understanding.

*Captain Boring,* she thought, stifling a laugh.

"What?" Lexa asked, swirling the ice in her glass. "What's so funny?"

"Nothing," Ariana said. "Just thinking about how everything's falling into place."

And not just for Lexa and Palmer and her and Jasper. Already tonight Ariana had met several influential Stone and Grave alumni who worked in a number of different and fascinating fields. All of them had attended Ivy League schools, and three people had already offered to write her recommendations for Princeton. The whole world was opening up at Ariana's feet. In two year's time she would be a freshman at Princeton University, just as she'd always dreamed. She might have fallen a couple of years behind schedule, thanks to Reed Brennan, but she would get there. All she had to be was patient. And patience was something Ariana had in spades. How else could she have survived those eighteen months inside the Brenda T.?

Suddenly the crowd before her parted, and there was Jasper. It was the first time she'd seen him all night, and he put all the other boys to shame in his black tux and long dark gray tie. He looked elegant, sleek, sophisticated. And he had an incredibly sexy look on his face as he approached. A look that said he knew something no one else in the room knew.

That he knew her.

"Hi, ladies," he said, hands in his pockets as he paused in front of them.

Ariana's heart was on fire.

"Hi, Jasper," Lexa said in a friendly way. "You look quite dashing."

"You're looking lovely, too, Madame President," he said with a smile. Lexa blushed, and Ariana felt momentarily envious. But then he turned his eyes to her. "But, if you don't mind my saying so, nothing compares to my fellow pledge."

Ariana smiled and cast her eyes at the ground.

"I don't mind at all," Lexa said, accustomed to the flirtatious ways of the boys at APH. "I happen to agree."

"*Do* you now?" Jasper asked, his face lighting up. "That's very interesting." He turned around, kicking his heel against the floor, and leaned back next to Ariana. "You know, you two will *never* believe what I heard about you the other day."

Ariana glanced at Lexa and watched as all the blood instantly drained from her face. She wanted to reach for her friend's wrist, to reassure her that there was nothing Jasper could possibly know, but before she could, he continued.

"I heard that the two of you have been very . . . bad . . . girls," he said, leaning toward them, his eyes gleaming with mischief.

Ariana's mouth went dry. He couldn't. He didn't. "What . . . what do you mean?" she asked, the smile frozen on her face.

"Don't you two know by now?" he teased. "It's impossible to keep secrets around here."

Ariana's eyes darted to Lexa, who looked like she was about to faint. She felt as if her own heart was being twisted into a coil, tightening, tightening, tightening with each passing second. There was no way he could possibly know. There was just no way.

"I—"

She had to say something. Anything that made sense. But she

could think of nothing. What was she supposed to say to that? What was he thinking? How could he know?

Without another word, Jasper turned and sauntered off, disappearing into the crowd. That was when Lexa started choking.

"Lexa!" Ariana hissed, whirling to her friend. Lexa pounded on her own chest with a flat hand and turned toward the bar, dropping her glass on the wood surface, where it promptly spilled. "Lexa, are you choking?"

Lexa managed to shake her head no, but she gripped the bar with both hands, coughing like mad and making awful, strangled sounds.

"Stop! Lexa! Stop and breathe!" Ariana said, wrapping her arm around her friend and looking around at the Stone and Grave alums apologetically. Any second someone was going to shout for help, and they'd have a dozen of the nation's finest physicians all over them. Ariana didn't need that kind of attention on Lexa. Not right now. Not when she was clearly spiraling all over again.

"Breathe, Lex. Just breathe," Ariana said in her ear.

Finally, finally, Lexa stopped coughing. Holding her arms around Lexa's slim shoulders, Ariana glanced around wildly, desperate to find Jasper in the crowd—desperate to hunt him down and make him explain.

"Oh my God, he knows," Lexa hissed, her voice raspy. "He knows, Ana. How does he know?"

The bartender gave Lexa a disturbed, curious look, and Ariana's blood turned to ice.

"Lexa, shut up," she said through her teeth.

But inside, her own voice was in complete panic. *He does. He does know. But how? How and why? Why him? Why is this happening to me? Why* him?

Lexa promptly began to cry. Ariana grabbed her by the shoulders and forced her to face her, channeling all her frustration, all her anger, all her fear, into controlling her friend.

"Lexa, stop," she said, looking into her friend's eyes. Her skin was an awful grayish color, as if all the blood had left her body. "We don't know what he was talking about."

Except that she did know what he was talking about. Because what else could it be? What else could he know?

But how? How? How the hell did he *know*?

"I'm going to go find him and talk to him, okay?" Ariana said. Her voice cracked, and she gritted her teeth. Weakness was not an option. Not now.

Ariana glanced at the nearby cliques and klatches, looking for Soomie, Maria, Tahira, Conrad . . . anyone who could come hang out with Lexa. Anyone who could keep her focused and in the now. But she saw only strangers. Her eyes darted toward the doorway that led to the hall and the bathroom beyond. Grasping Lexa's arm, she steered her across the room and out the door. The bathroom had been built for parties, with a lounge area just outside the toilet. Ariana shot a stiff smile at the elderly woman in front of the mirror, before flinging Lexa inside the private room and closing the door behind them. Lexa sat right down on the closed toilet and put her head in her hands. "You stay here and calm down. Lock the door behind me and don't move. Do you understand me?"

Slowly, silently, Lexa nodded.

"Everything is going to be fine," Ariana promised Lexa, crouching down and whispering the words in her ear. "I'm going to fix this. Just . . . don't do anything stupid."

When she stood up again, Lexa looked up, directly into her eyes. Ariana took a breath. Lexa was not gone. She was still with her. This could be fixed. It had to be fixed.

"I will be right back," Ariana assured her. "Promise me you won't move. Promise."

"I promise," Lexa said.

That was all Ariana needed to hear, and she was off. Off to keep the love of her life from repeating what he knew. By any means necessary.

# OBLITERATED

Jasper was here somewhere. In this room, among these people. These people she needed to impress. These people who could make her future. These people who, moments ago, had seemed like the answer to everything. They'd seemed like family, like openly helpful new friends. But now they were all potential enemies. Because Jasper could tell any of them the secret that could end her life.

Ariana whirled around the room, in search of that familiar head of blond hair. Everywhere, everywhere, everywhere there was nothing but black, white, and gray. Tuxedo after tuxedo, gown after gown, curious face after curious face. Somewhere nearby someone let forth a loud, belly laugh. Laughter. So out of place. So wrong. They were mocking her. Every one of them. Staring at her, staring through her, knowing her, mocking her.

Where *was* he? He was hiding from her on purpose. She could feel it. Hiding from her and torturing her. Making her search. Making her desperate. Making her weak. But why?

Why was he doing this to her? He'd said he loved her. That he would always love her, no matter what. How could he have found out? How could he possibly know?

And then, suddenly, Ariana stopped. Right in the center of the marble floor, she simply froze. Her lack of movement was so sudden that a waiter almost tripped over her. He apologized and kept moving, straightening the empty glasses on his tray, but Ariana barely noticed. Because suddenly, she knew. Suddenly she understood.

The soccer game. The soccer game had been very illuminating. Now she knew what that meant. It meant that he had somehow found out the truth about her there. That she, her identity, her worst secret, had been illuminated. But how?

A photo suddenly flashed through her mind. A picture of young Reed Brennan chasing a soccer ball across a verdant field. Reed . . . soccer . . . Reed . . . soccer. It all made sense.

A chill coursed through her body, and Ariana hugged herself.

Jasper's game had been at Georgetown Prep. Reed Brennan must have been there. Maybe she was scouting for her team or something? Who knew? Who cared? She had been there. And she had spoken to Jasper. And Jasper had told her all about the new girl with the ice-blue eyes, and Reed had started to talk. Talk all about the girl *she* had once known with ice-blue eyes. The two of them had talked and talked and figured it all out, and now Jasper knew. It was just as it had been with Thomas Pearson. The moment she found herself in love—real, true love—Reed came along to obliterate it.

Reed Brennan had ruined her. Again.

But how had he found out about Lexa? About Kaitlynn's death? That part made zero sense.

"Champagne, miss?"

Ariana jolted out of her paranoid reverie. She took a glass from the offered tray, downed it in one gulp, then grabbed two more. The waiter was obviously startled, but said nothing. Quickly Ariana moved toward the glass wall closest to her, tripping over someone's strappy heel as she went. She muttered an apology and kept moving. The entire room was spinning, which made it difficult to focus, but she made it to the wall. She pressed her back against the cold glass and downed the second flute of champagne.

Taking a deep breath, she placed the empty glass on a table and held the third. She watched the happy faces of her peers as they hobnobbed with the elite of Stone and Grave, and slowly, slowly, she started to come back to herself. She could not let Reed Brennan do this to her. Not again. Reed had nothing to do with her. Nothing to do with Briana Leigh Covington.

She would not allow Reed to ruin this life too.

Ariana looked down at the full glass of champagne. She scoffed, disgusted with herself, and set it aside. Now was not the time to start drinking. Now was not the time to lose control. She was going to need all of her faculties if she was going to survive what was going to happen next. What had to happen.

Clenching her jaw, Ariana pushed herself away from the wall. She sidled through the room slowly now, methodically, checking each group of revelers one by one by one.

And then, finally, she found him. She felt a pang of sadness, a pang of nostalgia, a pang of real loss, as she watched him laugh with a pair of older men. And then she shoved it all aside and made her move. She walked up behind him and whispered in his ear.

"Come with me," she said huskily, determinedly.

Jasper, ever so languidly, smiled. He looked at the older men, who both gazed upon her with leering, sparkling eyes. "Duty calls, gents."

They both nodded in understanding, which made Ariana's blood curdle. But she ignored it. She had to. She had far more important things to deal with. She turned and lifted her chin and, smiling blithely at the illustrious guests as she passed them by—smiling as if she had no idea who Jasper was or that he was eagerly following her— she slowly led him away.

# OVER

Ariana shut the heavy wooden door of what must have once been the potting shed. Long shelves lined two of the walls, all of which were empty. There was a low metal counter along the third wall, a large sink dead center, its tall faucet turned to the side. Above this hung a series of metal pegs, and from those pegs dangled dozens of gardening tools. Spades and shovels in various sizes, rakes and hoes and forks, and several pairs of clippers and shears. The tile floor had been swept clean of dirt and potting soil, and the air inside was frigidly cold, as if the heat hadn't been turned on in years.

"Hey," Jasper said, turning to her suddenly. So suddenly she almost stepped on his toes. Their knees bumped, and Ariana felt a surge of attraction followed by a hatred so white hot she could hardly keep herself from screeching. "You sure you don't want Lexa to join us?"

And just like that, Ariana snapped. She closed her hand around his throat and backed him into the shelves behind him, so hard she slammed the back of his head against an edge.

"Ow! Sonofabitch!" he shouted. He pushed her away with both hands. "What the hell was that?"

"What do you know?" Ariana demanded, her chest heaving.

Jasper laughed. He touched his hand to the back of his head, then checked his fingers for blood. "God, Ana. If you like it rough, you could have just told me."

"Shut up!" Ariana turned and grabbed the first pair of shears she saw. The blades were at least a foot long and rusty, their tips still crusted with dirt. Jasper's eyes suddenly widened, and he backed into the shelves again. "What do you know!?" she demanded. She stepped right up to him and held the sharp tip of the blade right beneath his chin. Jasper tilted his head back, his Adam's apple bobbing up and down as he eyed the shears with terror.

Yet still, he laughed. "Okay, calm down. Calm down," he said, raising his hands in surrender. "There was this guy at the game . . . he went to your old school."

"A guy?" Ariana demanded, confused.

"Yeah. Glenn or something. No . . . Gray . . . ?"

"Gage?" Ariana demanded, pressing the blades into his skin. "Was it Gage?"

"No, no! It was definitely Glenn something or other," Jasper said, panicked. "He told me about the affair you had with your professor last year," he said in a rush. "Your *female* professor."

Ariana blinked. Sweat had popped out along her lip and under her arms, even in the freezing-cold room. What the hell was Jasper talking about? Last year she'd been at the Brenda T. She'd had no professors, let alone female ones, let alone female ones with whom she'd had an affair.

"Ana? Can you let me go now?" Jasper asked.

Ana.

Ana Covington.

Briana Leigh Covington. Of course. Jasper wasn't talking about Gage Coolidge. He wasn't even talking about Ariana Osgood. He was talking about Briana Leigh. The real Briana Leigh. Of course.

Slowly, Ariana dropped the shears. They hit the ground with a clatter.

"The affair," she heard herself say. "The affair I had with a female professor."

Jasper stood up straight and cleared his throat. He shifted the knot of his tie. "Yeah. Some woman named Miss French?" he said. "And I just thought . . . I don't know . . . since you and Lexa have been spending so much time together lately . . ."

"You thought Lexa and I were having an affair?" Ariana asked.

"I don't know. Not really," Jasper said. "I was just messing with you. Not that, I mean, if you are, I want to make it perfectly clear that I'm totally okay with that."

Ariana's shoulders slumped. Suddenly she felt exhausted. So exhausted she could hardly stand. She leaned back against the cold metal sink and put her face in her hands. Jasper didn't know anything. Not one single thing. She should have been relieved. She *would* have been, if she hadn't just threatened the life of the boy she loved with a pair of rusty old pruning shears.

"Um, Ana?" Jasper asked. "Can I ask you a question?"

With a sigh, Ariana dropped her hands. She looked up at him, at his innocent, questioning face, and knew it was all over. Knew that she might still have to kill him. Because he'd seen her. The worst of her. And now, he'd be suspicious. Now he'd question everything about her.

Everything, everything, *everything* hinged on whatever he said next.

"If I promise to never piss you off again, will you promise to never wield sharp objects at my throat again?" he said.

And, just like that, Ariana started to laugh.

Jasper took a step toward her, and Ariana, full of relief and love, was about to fall into his arms—fall into his arms and kiss him like nothing else mattered—when there was a crash. It was a crash so huge, so startlingly loud, so never-ending, that Ariana was certain the entire greenhouse had just collapsed atop all her friends.

And then there was a scream. One long, piercing, wailing scream.

Ariana whirled for the door. She shoved through the wall of men in front of her, gaping up at the huge, yawning hole in the roof of the greenhouse. It looked as if a boulder had fallen through the glass. Giant shards jutted out toward the opening, and several pieces dangled precariously, ready to fall onto the crowd below at any moment. What had fallen through the roof? A tree? A meteor? What could possibly make a hole that big? Ariana's heart was in her throat. If Lexa wasn't freaking before, this would end her.

Just as she had this thought, she arrived at the center of the crowd, which had formed a circle on the marble floor. Ariana stopped in her tracks and grabbed Jasper's arm to keep from going down—from collapsing in shock. It appeared that she was wrong. Lexa wasn't going to be ended by the sight of all the broken glass. Because Lexa lay in the center of the floor, blood pouring from one ear, glass all around her, with Maria, Soomie, Tahira, Palmer, Rob, and Conrad kneeling all around her.

# NEVER SAW IT COMING

*This is my fault. I did this. This is all my fault.*

Ariana rushed into the emergency room after her friends. Palmer gripped her hand as they followed Soomie and Landon to the admitting desk. Maria had ridden in the ambulance with Lexa, who, miraculously, was still alive. At least, she had been when they'd wheeled her stretcher out of the greenhouse.

"Where is she!?"

Ariana whirled around to find Senator and Mrs. Greene barreling through the door. Mrs. Greene was dressed in a royal blue ball gown, her husband in tails. Clearly they had been attending a formal function this evening as well.

"Mrs. Greene, I'm so sorry," Soomie said, tears streaming down her face as she approached. Hunter came with her, looking ashen under his lank hair.

Ariana's heart stopped beating. Did they know something new? Had Lexa . . . died?

"She . . . she tried to kill herself," Soomie said. "We didn't even realize she was gone. She must have gone upstairs . . . Maria's bedroom . . . one of the windows overlooks the greenhouse and she . . . she jumped."

"Omigod!" Mrs. Greene covered her mouth with one hand.

"Is she going to be okay?" Palmer asked.

"We don't know. They won't tell us anything," Soomie said with a sob.

Mrs. Greene went right for the desk, her husband in tow.

"Where is she? Where's my baby?" she demanded of the overwhelmed clerk. "Take me to see her now."

Ariana, unable to take it any longer, fell into the nearest chair. Palmer sat next to her, on the edge of his own seat, rubbing her back mechanically.

"It's okay. It's going to be okay," he said.

"You don't know that," Ariana snapped, past being polite.

Palmer didn't seem to notice, however. He stared at the crowd near the desk as if trying to read their lips. Jasper walked in and sat down at Ariana's other side.

"I'll be right back," Palmer said. "I'm gonna see if I can find out what's going on."

The second he was gone, Jasper took her hand. "I'm here," he said. "I'm here, Ana."

She turned and looked at him. "This is my fault," she said aloud.

PURE SIN 191

"I should have been there with her. I should have protected her. I should have done a better job."

"What are you talking about?" Jasper said. "You couldn't have stopped her."

"I could have," Ariana said. "I should have. I should have seen this coming. I—"

Suddenly Ariana's words died in her throat. Her mouth snapped shut. The entire world faded to gray around her. Jasper wasn't there. Palmer wasn't there. Soomie and Hunter and Rob and Tahira and Mr. and Mrs. Greene. The boy with the broken arm, the woman in labor in the corner, the young girl holding her head in her hands, all of them were gone.

All there was in the world was Reed Brennan. Reed Brennan, Reed Brennan, Reed Brennan.

Reed Brennan, who was standing not twenty feet away.

CHARMING GIRLS.
FINE BREEDING.
PERFECT MANNERS.
BLACK MAGIC.

THE BILLINGS SCHOOL,
ESTABLISHED 1915,
WHERE THE GIRLS ARE WITCHES.

TURN THE PAGE FOR
A SNEAK PEEK OF

THE BOOK OF SPELLS
*a private prequel*

Even at the tender age of sixteen, Elizabeth Williams was the rare girl who knew her mind. She knew she preferred summer to all other seasons. She knew she couldn't stand the pink and yellow floral wallpaper the decorator had chosen for her room. She knew that she would much rather spend time with her blustery, good-natured father than her ever-critical, humorless mother—though the company of either was difficult to come by. And she knew, without a shadow of a doubt, that going away to the Billings School for Girls was going to be the best thing that ever happened to her.

As she sat in the cushioned seat of her bay window overlooking sun-streaked Beacon Hill, she folded her dog-eared copy of *The Jungle* in her lap, making sure to keep her finger inside to hold her place. She placed her feet up on the pink cushions, new buckled shoes and all, and pressed her temple against the warm glass with a wistful sigh. It was September 1915, and Boston was experiencing an Indian summer, with temperatures scorching the sidewalks and causing the new automobiles to sputter and die along the sides of the roads. Eliza would have given anything to be back at the Cape house, running along the shoreline in her bathing clothes, splashing in the waves, her swim cap forgotten and her dark hair tickling her shoulders. But instead, here she was, buttoned into a stiff, green cotton dress her mother had picked out for her, the wide, white collar scratching her neck. Any minute now, Maurice would bring the coach around and squire her off to the train station, where she and her maid, Renee, would board a train for Easton, Connecticut, and the Billings School. The moment she got to her room in Crenshaw House, she was going to change into her most comfortable linen dress, jam her floppy brown hat over her hair, and set out in search of the library. Because living at a school more than two hours away from home meant that her mother couldn't control her. Couldn't criticize her. Couldn't nitpick every little thing she wore, every book she read, every choice she made. Being away at school meant freedom.

Of course Eliza's mother had other ideas. If her wishes came true, Billings would turn Eliza into a true lady. Eliza would catch herself a worthy husband, and she would return home by Christmas triumphantly engaged, just as her sister May had.

After two years at Billings, eighteen-year-old May was now an engaged woman—and engaged to a Thackery, no less. George Thackery III of the Thackery tanning fortune. She'd come home in June, diamond ring and all, and was now officially their mother's favorite—though truly she had been so all along.

Suddenly the thick oak door of Eliza's private bedroom opened and in walked her mother, Rebecca Cornwall Williams. Her blond hair billowed like a cloud around her head and her stylish, ankle-length gray skirt tightened her steps. She wore a matching tassel-trimmed jacket over her dress, even in this ridiculous heat, and had the Williams pearls, as always, clasped around her throat. As she entered, her eyes flicked over Eliza and her casual posture with exasperation. Eliza quickly sat up, smoothed her skirt, straightened her back, and attempted to tuck her book behind her.

"Hello, Mother," she said with the polished politeness that usually won over the elder Williams. "How are you this morning?"

Her mother's discerning blue eyes narrowed as she walked toward her daughter.

"Your sister and I are going to shop for wedding clothes. We've come to say our good-byes," she said formally.

Out in the hallway, May hovered, holding her tan leather gloves and new brimless hat at her waist. May's blond hair was pulled back in a stylish chignon, which complimented her milky skin and round, rosy cheeks. Garnets dangled from her delicate earlobes. She always looked elegant, even for a simple day of shopping.

Eliza's mother leaned down and snatched the book right out from under Eliza's skirt.

"*The Jungle*?" she said, holding the book between her thumb and forefinger. "Elizabeth, you cannot be seen reading this sort of rot at Billings. Modern novels are not proper reading for a young lady. Especially not a Williams."

Eliza's gaze flicked to her sister, who quickly looked away. A few years ago, May would have defended Eliza's literary choices, but not since her engagement. For the millionth time Eliza wondered how May could have changed so much. When she'd gone away to school she'd been adventurous, tomboyish, sometimes even brash. It was as if falling in love had lobotomized her sister. If winning a diamond ring from a boy meant forgetting who she was, then Eliza was determined to die an old maid.

"Headmistress Almay has turned out some of the finest ladies of society, and I intend for you to be one of them," Eliza's mother continued.

*What about what I intend?* Eliza thought.

"And you won't be bringing this. I don't want the headmistress thinking she's got a daydreamer on her hands." Her mother turned and tossed Eliza's book into the crate near the door—the one piled with old toys and dresses meant for the hospital bazaar her mother was helping to plan.

Eliza looked down at the floor, her eyes aflame and full of tears. Then her mother did something quite unexpected. She clucked her tongue and ran her hands from Eliza's shoulders down her arms until they were firmly holding her hands. Eliza couldn't remember the last time her mother had touched her.

"Come now. Let me look at you," her mother said.

Eliza raised her chin and looked her mother in the eye. The older woman tilted her head and looked Eliza over. She nudged a stray hair behind Eliza's ear, tucking it deftly into her updo. Then she straightened the starched white collar on her traveling dress.

"This green really does bring out your eyes," she mused. "You are a true beauty, Eliza. Never underestimate yourself."

An unbearable thickness filled Eliza's throat. Part of her wanted to thank her mother for saying something so very kind, while another part of her wanted to shout that her entire life was not going to be built around her beauty—that she hoped to be known for something more. But neither sentiment left her tongue, and silence reigned in the warm, pink room.

"May. The book," her mother said suddenly, snapping her fingers.

Startled, May slipped a book from the hall table where it had been hidden from view, and took a step into the room to hand it to her mother.

"This is for you, Eliza," her mother said, holding the book out. "A going-away gift."

Silently, Eliza accepted the gorgeous sandalwood leather book with both hands, relishing the weight of it. She opened the cover, her eyes falling on the thick parchment pages. They were blank. She looked up at her mother questioningly.

"Today is the beginning of a whole new life, Eliza," her mother said. "You're going to want to remember every moment . . . and I hope you'll remember home when you write in it as well."

Eliza hugged the book to her chest. "Thank you, Mother," she said.

"Now remember, May is one of Billings's most revered graduates," she said, her tone clipped once again. "You have a lot to live up to, Elizabeth. Don't disappoint me."

Then she leaned in and gave Eliza a brief, dry kiss on the forehead.

Eliza rolled her blue eyes as her mother shuffled back down the hall. Then she bent to pluck her book from the trash, but froze when something caught her eye: May still hovering in the hallway.

"May?" Eliza said. Usually her sister trailed her mother like the tail of a comet.

May looked furtively down the hall after their mother, then took a step toward Eliza's open door. There was something about her manner that set the tiny hairs on Eliza's neck on end.

"May, what is it?" Eliza asked, her pulse beginning to race.

"I just wanted to tell you . . . about Billings . . . about Crenshaw House," May whispered, leaning into the doorjamb. "Eliza . . . there's something you need to know."

"What?" Eliza asked, breathless. "What is it?"

"May Williams! I'm waiting!" their mother called from the foot of the stairs.

May started backward. "Oh, I must go."

Eliza grabbed her sister's wrist.

"May, please. I'm your sister. If there's something you need to tell me—"

May covered Eliza's hand with her own and looked up into her eyes. "Just promise me you'll be careful," she said earnestly, her blue eyes shining. "Promise me, Eliza, that you'll be safe."

Eliza blinked. "Of course, May. Of course I'll be safe. What could possibly harm me at a place like Billings?"

The sound of hurried footsteps on the stairs stopped them both.

Renee rushed into view, holding her skirts up, her eyes wide with terror. The sort of terror only Rebecca Williams could inspire in her servants.

"May! Your mother is fit to burst," she said through her teeth. "Mind your manners and get downstairs now."

A tortured noise sounded from the back of May's throat. Then she quickly gave Eliza a kiss on the cheek, squeezing her hands tightly. "I love you, Eliza. Always remember that. No matter what happens."

Then she released Eliza and was gone.

MEET THE ORIGINAL BILLINGS GIRLS IN

THE BOOK OF SPELLS

COMING DECEMBER 2010